Fires
Book 1

A Thread of Time

By

J. Naomi Ay

Published by Ayzenberg, Inc
Copyright 2015-2016 Ayzenberg, Inc.

040216

Cover Design by Amy Jambor
Cover art dleindecp@depositphotos.com & gertot1967@depositphotos.com

Also by
J. Naomi Ay

Firesetter series
A Thread of Time (Book 1)
Amyr's Command (Book 2)
Three Kings (Book 3)
Exceeding Expectations (Book 4)

The Two Moons of Rehnor series
The Boy who Lit up the Sky (Book 1)
My Enemy's Son (Book 2)
Of Blood and Angels (Book 3)
Firestone Rings (Book 4)
The Days of the Golden Moons (Book 5)
Golden's Quest (Book 6)
Metamorphosis (Book 7)
The Choice (Book 8)
Treasure Hunt (Book 9)
Space Chase (Book 10)
Imperial Masquerade (Book 11)
Rivalry (Book 12)
Thirteen (Book 13)
Betrayal (Book 14)
Fairy Tales (Book 15)
Gone for a Spin (Book 16)

Table of Contents

Chapter 1 – Lance
Chapter 2 – Jan
Chapter 3 – Ailana
Chapter 4 – Lance
Chapter 5 – Jan
Chapter 6 – Pellen
Chapter 7 – Ailana
Chapter 8 – Jan
Chapter 9 – Ailana
Chapter 10 – Lance
Chapter 11 – Pellen
Chapter 12 – Ailana
Chapter 13 – Dov
Chapter 14 – Rekah
Chapter 15 – Lance
Chapter 16 – Rekah
Chapter 17 – Jan
Chapter 18 – Ailana
Chapter 19 – Sandy
Chapter 20 – Ailana
Chapter 21 – Dov
Chapter 22 – Ailana
Chapter 23 – Dov
Chapter 24 – Ailana
Chapter 25 – Lance

Chapter 1
Lance

I joined the Allied SpaceForce for one reason and one reason alone, I was flat broke and I needed money. After hocking everything I owned at the local pawnshop, or selling it on Craigslist, I was down to forty-three dollars and thirty-seven cents, in addition to the ancient Euro my father had left me as an inheritance.

"What the heck is this?" I had mumbled, holding the single coin in my palm, while at the same time, the lawyer was informing my brother, Hank that he was bequeathed everything else in my father's estate.

Granted, Dad was no billionaire. His estate was pretty simple, a modest house in a not-so-great town, in the center of the continent, affectionately referred to as *The Armpit*. Still, it was worth something, and undoubtedly, more than this useless coin. I mean, a Euro? Europe hadn't existed for several centuries!

"Ha!" Hank had laughed in his annoying nasally voice, gloating over his victory in this final round of the sibling game. Yep. Dad loved him best, and that was now proven without a doubt. I was the loser when it came to paternal affection.

"Congratulations," the lawyer said to Hank, but not to me.

Hank nodded regally, savoring his win. Had the lawyer not been there, my brother would have left with a minimum of a bloody nose and a maximum of a five month stay in traction.

"I'll just have you sign off on the deed." The lawyer presented the documents to Hank as I rose from my seat, flipping my precious antique Euro coin between my fingers. "Good luck, Lance. Hank, let me take you out to lunch." The lawyer scumbag barely glanced in my direction, as I let myself out.

"Good riddance."

I didn't really blame him. He knew this cow was dry. He'd milk no costly legal fees from me and therefore, I didn't merit even a handshake.

Stepping out into the street, after leaving the dark and overly air conditioned building, I was momentarily blinded by the sudden burst of sunlight. I thought the crosswalk light was in my favor. I thought there were no vehicles on the street and the heat that was washing over me was merely the sun, while that roaring sound was a bus on the next corner. I thought wrong on all four counts. The next thing I knew, I was bouncing off the hood of something, only to end up beneath its wheels. Fortunately, by this point, I wasn't awake.

Three days later, I was, and less than delighted to discover I was in traction, the sort that I had wished upon Hank. Karma could sure be a bitch.

When my brother came to visit me in the hospital, sitting by my bedside and describing in great detail the renovations he was going to make to Dad's house, if I could have, I would have reached up and smacked him. Alternately, I would have yanked his tongue from his mouth, or removed his eyeballs from their sockets with my fingernails. As I couldn't lift a finger, and was far too drugged to even spit in his direction, I lay there prone, subjected to yet another round of fraternal gloating.

Six months passed until my back was more or less healed and I was released from the hospital, a new, but not improved man. I was also totally broke, so much in debt that four lifetimes of delivering pizzas, my previous occupation, wouldn't yield enough to ever make me a free man.

Briefly, I considered stepping into the street again and encouraging another vehicle to roll over me, this time finishing the job completely. That was the only way I could foresee escaping the hospital's payment plan, which as I departed, was detailed on an invoice that would follow me for the next forty years.

Instead, I headed to a local pub where I spent the next day and night drowning my sorrows in beer, drinking up what little remained of my money. It was stupid, of course. I should have put it toward the hospital's first installment. Somehow, and at some point, I managed to stagger home to my flat, where fortunately, the landlord had taken pity upon me during my absence.

Gloria didn't evict me, or toss my things in the street during my convalescence. This could have been entirely due to the fact that no one else was willing to rent that dive. It also could have been because she liked me. Poor Gloria was on the wrong side of forty, nearly twenty years my senior and throughout her life, had a habit of selecting the wrong kind of guy. This included me.

I regretted what happened. I became a whore. While I scrambled to pay the hospital bill by selling my stuff and raising money in any way I could, I kept Gloria entertained in exchange for the rent.

Every month, on the first, it went like this. Gloria would knock on my door, usually bright and early, undoubtedly, waking me from a sound and contented sleep that was much nicer than my reality. Groggily, I'd stumble from the sofa, swing the door wide open to admit her and feign surprise at her arrival during this ungodly hour.

"The rent, Lance," she'd say frostily, holding out a hand, the other knuckled into her side, a foot tapping out an impatient rhythm. "I can't let you go another month without paying."

"Rent," I'd mutter sleepily, running a hand across my night's beard. "Oh. Gloria. Yeah, the thing is---"

"What?"

"I'm a little short again this month." I'd pat my hands against my hips as if checking inside the nonexistent pockets of my marginally clean and slightly torn boxer shorts.

"Mhm," she'd mutter, her eyes drawn to my hands, where inevitably she'd find a prime example of morning wood. "Oh. Is that for me?"

"It's all I've got right now," I'd say, which was followed by the old couch being cleared of my ratty blanket and the even older sleeper mattress beneath extended to its full size.

Then, I did what I did best, because at twenty-four, I was a loser at every other round in this game of life. Gloria left happy, and my lack of rent was forestalled for another month.

Eventually, Gloria tired of this game, or maybe, she preferred to play it instead with the guy in the apartment across the hall. At any rate, she gave me an ultimatum. At the end of the month, pay up or get out.

"You got anything else?" the pawnbroker asked, as I stared at the measly number written on my ticket.

"Hey, that ring is worth more than that!" I insisted. "It was my mother's. She left it to me to give to my future wife."

"I'm doing you a favor then," the guy replied. "You give a girl this piece of crap cubic zirconia and she's liable to throw it back at you and walk out of your wedding."

"It's not a fake."

"Listen to me, son. I've seen a lot of rings in my day, and that one's about as real as my tooth." He proceeded to reach into his mouth and pull out a shiny, white incisor. "Look's nice, eh? Indestructible, too. Better than the real thing, but my wife doesn't wear it on her finger. So, you got anything else for me to look at?"

I would have liked to offer him my fist, but I didn't. Since Gloria dumped me, this guy was about the only friend I had. Putting my hands in my pockets to restrain them, I pretended to consider the paltry offer on my mother's ring. I was going to take it. I had no choice. I was down to my last nickel, or rather, the forty-three dollars and thirty-seven cents which were already promised to the hospital.

"Just this," I said, finding that stupid Euro coin in my pocket. "Maybe this is a collector's item?"

"Let me see." The guy dropped his loop over his eye and turned the coin this way and that way. He murmured something, while trying to read it. "I don't know what in the hell this says. It's a piece of crap.

Not worth a nickel." He tossed it back, whereupon it rolled the distance of the counter, before falling flat.

Heads. Some dude in a crown looked off across the horizon at the ancient toasters and television sets with orange price tags hanging from them.

"It's an ancient Euro."

"No, it's not. What language does that look like to you?"

"I don't know. Greek? Russian? Portuguese?"

The pawnbroker shook his head and glanced at the door. Another customer had come in, or more likely, another victim of the decrepit economy came to hock whatever he had in order to eat. "Are you taking my offer on the ring, or no?"

"I guess so," I said, studying my not-Euro coin again. "You sure this isn't worth anything?"

"Not to me."

"That's worth a fair amount in the old Empire," the new customer interrupted. "Although, it'll cost you a heck of a lot more to travel the ten lightyears to get there."

"Where?"

I turned to look at my neighbor, only to discover he was wearing a SpaceForce uniform and carrying an old iPad from the twenty-first century.

"I found this in a rummage sale on Darius II. Is it worth anything, Pops?" He set it on the counter for the old man, and then, held out his hand to take a look at my coin. "Yep, this is an old Imperial dollar. It's definitely worth something to collectors around the galaxy. It dates back to the reign of the Great Emperor. That's who this guy is on the front. You wouldn't want to sell it to me, would you?"

"I will buy it first," the pawnbroker interjected.

"No way." I snatched it back from the spandex-clad spaceman. "You can buy his iPad, Pops. You missed your chance with me."

Grabbing my mom's cubic zirconia wedding ring off the counter as well, I left the pawnshop with a new spring in my step. I was determined to take my coin to a place where its value would be appreciated. Worth something could mean several thousand and several thousand would easily pay off the hospital bill. This coin would give me a chance to restart my life debt-free. On the other hand, if I had to take the coin across the galaxy, why would I bother coming back?

Unfortunately, the fare on a spaceplane to the nearest port where the coin could be exchanged, cost more than I would have gained selling the ring and the clothing off my back, as well as the old sofa, and the toaster in my flat. The only way to get myself from here to there was to get on a ship that didn't cost me anything.

"The dude's spandex uniform wasn't all that ugly," I told myself, walking into the SpaceForce recruiting office down the street. "And, I'd get three squares a day, a hot shower, and a clean bed without any aging landladies in it." That didn't sound a whole lot different than prison, but at that point, I didn't care.

An hour later, I walked out, officially a recruit with a contract in hand, and an induction physical scheduled for the following day.

Chapter 2
Jan

I wasn't meant to venture anywhere beyond my little village, and neither did I wish too. Unlike my older brother, who dreamed of adventures on faraway planets, I was content to keep my feet firmly planted on the sunlit planet. I loved the sea, though, the calm rolling of the ocean waves, and the wind, which I imagined lovingly whispered my name.

My name was Jan, an ordinary, plain, single syllabic handle which should have been simple enough for anyone to pronounce. Like my name, my appearance varied from predominately dull to boring, depending who was judging it at that particular moment.

"Isn't Jan sweet," my mother would say, preferring to overlook my unremarkable appearance with blinded, maternal devotion.

At the same moment, my brother, Taul might proclaim my face homelier than his pet frog, a mummified creature which had grown only uglier since it had died several years prior.

I had never understood the comparison to the frog, as my hair was not green, but a nearly white blonde, bearing only a hint more color than the snow white cloud of my advanced years. My eyes were also pale, a clear, almost-colorless gray, providing no enhancement to my fair skin, while my body was equally as plain. As a young woman, I had the figure of a tall boy, with only tiny budding breasts, flat hips, and a waist, though slim, clearly without curves.

"Makeup," my mother insisted. "Cosmetics will do wonders for Jan. When she's old enough, twelve or thirteen, we ought cover her in mascara and dye her hair red."

Unfortunately, for my mother, I had no interest in enhancing my plainness, preferring instead the loneliness of my little boat, in which I would meander down the river, never quite reaching the sea, chasing the fish as they sought to run from my net.

When I was fourteen, my appearance no more improved than in my preteens, I acquired a friend, a boy much smaller than myself. One day, I discovered him sitting upon the dock, gazing curiously at my little boat. His small feet were hanging just above the water, bare of any shoes, his toenails cracked and dirty.

"Hey, get away from there," I called, immediately assuming the worst, for orphaned and homeless street urchins were prevalent during those times.

"Is it yours?" the boy asked, turning bright blue eyes upon me, his gaze so intense it momentarily threw me off guard.

"Yes," I snapped, upon recovering my senses. "Now, get away from it, you little thief."

"I'm not a thief. I was only looking at it. I wish I had a boat like this. I think I would love to sail."

"That's ridiculous." The child looked no more than eight years old and without a penny to his name, let alone a boat. "Go away."

I shoved him aside, although I didn't want to touch the child's filthy torn t-shirt or the sunburnt skin of the shoulders peeking through.

He shrugged, those red arms drifting up and down, his intense gaze and colorful eyes refusing to leave me in peace.

"How come you have a boat like this?" he asked, the innocent words drifting from lips my Aunt Ailana would have said were both as plump and red as a cherry, as becoming on this child as a woman fully grown.

"It was my father's," I replied, doing my best to ignore the little pest, and instead set about preparing my fishing nets, and the single sail which would take me from the shore.

Clipping the sail to the halyard, I laid the sheets where I could reach them with one hand. Since neither my mother nor Taul took to the sea, I had become quite proficient at guiding the tiller with one hand, while controlling the sail with the other.

"Would you like some help?" the boy asked, already rising to his feet, assuming his presence was desired. "I'd like to come, and I can help you sail, or row with your oars."

"No! Absolutely not. Go away."

Untying the bow line, I made haste to hurry away from this annoying child. The prow of my little craft swung outward.

"I can be useful," the boy insisted. "Please let me come with you."

I didn't deign to answer as I released my stern line and drifted off. I let the wind and current direct me onward, to the river and the hint of salt-filled air, the brief few hours of solitude, and the peace, as well as the dinner it would bring to me.

Unfortunately, my pleasure was all too brief. Though the sky had been clear at the outset of my adventure, only moments later, dark clouds swarmed overhead, accompanied by what would become torrents of rain. Quickly, I turned the boat homeward, now fighting the wind back to my dock, and the boy who sat waiting expectantly, his face inexplicably lighting with joy as I once again sailed into his midst.

"What are you going to do now?" he asked, rushing for my bow line and expertly tying it before I could think to refuse his aid.

"Go home, I suppose." I climbed on the foredeck and reversed all I had done less than an hour earlier, stowing my sail, and locking the single hatch.

"Oh." He gazed at me, the raindrops already dampening his hair, a golden mass of dirty wild curls that only made my tresses pale further in comparison.

"I suppose you want to come home with me," I pronounced, already half way off the dock. "I suppose you think my mother will feed you and give you a bed."

"I didn't…" he began, his small feet trailing after mine, two of his steps equaling every one I placed.

"Do you know how many orphaned waifs come to our house everyday?" I demanded, not slowing pace, nor daring to look back, and not wanting or expecting an answer to my question. That would only encourage him. If he saw a hint of pity in my eyes, he would think he had won, when in truth, my mother's reaction to his presence would only result in a tongue lashing for me. "Go away. You can't come with me. My mother will set the dog on you if you dare approach our door."

The boy continued to follow me, either pretending he hadn't heard, or didn't believe me, in which case, he would have been correct. We had no dog. However, my mother always threatened it, even if she had to fake a vicious growling or barking sound herself. Sometimes, I faked the barking, although my rendition sounded more like a cow. Still, it managed to rid our porch of wayward orphans and other people of the street.

"Like ants they are," my mother said. "Give one a crumb and in minutes, the entire colony will appear."

"What's your name?" the child asked, still following me, pestering me. "Mine is Dov. I can spell it, D-O-V."

I don't know why, but I stopped short right then, causing the boy to bump into my back.

"Dov?" I gasped. "How does a street urchin know how to spell?"

"I don't know," the boy shrugged. "I just do." Again, those red shoulders shifted up and down. He blinked rapidly, his lips forcing a tiny smile again. "Tell me your name so we can be friends."

"I don't want to be your friend." Immediately, I was filled with remorse for speaking so harshly to this poor lonely child.

The rain was coming hard then and I was growing wet and cold. I longed to return home, to the warm fire in our hearth and hopefully, the remains of a hot cabbage soup, the last from my mother's kitchen garden.

"I mean," I continued, doing my best to explain in a way the young child would understand. "I am much older than you. It wouldn't be right. Now, for the last time, go on. Go away. I don't want you following me, and I can't give you anything or help you, in any case. Goodbye Dov." I waggled a finger at the road, before putting my fists on my hips and tapping my foot with impatience.

"But, I don't want your help," the boy insisted, refusing to acknowledge my dismissal, while the rain showered us from above. His wild curls became twisted ropes, and his thin, torn clothing clung to his tiny body.

"Then, what do you want from me?"

I never heard his answer. Lightning crackled and flashed directly over our heads, sending us scurrying into the doorway of the nearby abandoned building. We were lucky we had done so, for only a moment later, the ground rumbled with a sound akin to thunder as heavy trucks rolled down the road.

"It's them," I gasped, instinctively reaching for Dov's arm. Whether I did this to shelter him or protect myself, I wasn't certain. In any case, I pulled him down, the two of us squeezing into the furthest, darkest corner, cowering against the cracked glass door, hiding our faces and our hair beneath our arms. "Don't let them see us."

Dov didn't move. As far as I could tell, he never even breathed. For what seemed like the longest minute in my life, the two of us didn't exist.

Somewhere, further down the road, in the direction of the village market, I thought I heard screaming although it could have been the wind and rain. Somewhere, further down the road, I thought I heard the sound of gunshots, although it could have been the lightning, or the crackling of the fire as another abandoned building burst into flame.

Chapter 3
Ailana

On Saturdays, when I was a young woman, I helped my grandmother at her shop. She was a seamstress who spent her days tucking in or taking out, sewing buttons or hems, and occasionally, creating something all new from scratch. Sometimes, that something would be for me, even though most often, I didn't want it.

I didn't like my grandmother's creations then, and I didn't like having to sit next to her and sew stitches myself. I hadn't the patience to do such work and despite my best efforts, I generated only poor, pale copies of her handiwork.

Furthermore, Saturday was the best day of the week when all the other young people of our village would be resting or enjoying themselves instead of toiling. Yet, there I was, trapped in a dark and musty shop, next to an old, foul-mouthed woman who spent the entire time chiding my lackluster efforts.

"Not like that, Ailana," she'd snap, and in a swift swipe of a seam ripper, tear out everything I had just done. "You'll never get a job as a seamstress with such sloppy stitches."

"I don't want a job as a seamstress," I would retort, raising my chin, and thinking myself ever so clever.

"Too fine for such work, are you? Then, you shan't have this new dress. You are undeserving." She would hold up the golden gown with the handmade lace collar she had been tatting. "I shall have to give this to your cousin, Embo although she looks exactly like her mother, far too thin to fit it well, and with nothing to fill it up."

"Fine. Give it to her."

"Fine. I shall."

With the issue of the dress decided, I rethreaded my needle and attempted to hem the customer's skirt once again. It was a black sateen fabric that showed every misplaced needle-prick, too difficult a task for a novice such as me. Surely, my cousin Embo would have done a far better job. She always did, and Grandmother made certain I knew that.

"Your cousin will look like a shiny stick in this." Grandmother sniffed and sigh dramatically. "No amount of lace will make her appealing to a man. She's as plain and ordinary as a blank page, and this gold color will be dreadful with her pale skin, although I must say, she would do a much better job on that skirt than you."

"And, where is she today? Why isn't my cousin here suffering with me?"

"She is out looking for a man, no doubt, and having little luck in finding him."

Grandmother would snicker then, and I would do my best not to follow suit. I liked Embo well enough, although I tended to agree with Grandmother's assessment.

"You, on the other hand," Grandmother continued, "Would look lovely in this color, for your hair and complexion is the same as this gold thread.

Your face and especially, your smile would light it as if it was touched by a single ray from the sun. But, you are a spoiled rotten child, and undeserving of such a treasure. You also do not need it, for you can catch a man with just your face. Make your back stitch tighter, Ailana, or the hem will quickly pull out. Place it closer to the fabric's edge, else your stitches will show upon the skirt's face."

"Yes, Grandmother." I would sigh dramatically, too, and while tightening my back stitch, I'd avoid glancing in the direction of the golden dress.

I didn't want it anyway. It wasn't as if I was about to be invited to a palace ball. In this poor village full of those just like ourselves, it would look completely out of place.

"I once made this same dress for the little princess, Prince Mikal's daughter, although that one had pearl buttons all the way down the bodice here, instead of these plain gilt. Ach, the pearls were so much nicer. Did you know the Empress Sara had the exact same gown, and insisted her granddaughter's would match it in every detail?"

I did know about that dress, for I had heard this story many times before. During the old Empress's reign, Grandmother's shop was designated as an *Official Dressmaker* and a Royal Seal was placed upon the door. It was the only one so honored in our village, a tiny corner of the port city of Farku on the west coast of the continent that was called Mishnah. This was long ago, several decades past, although it felt like centuries to me.

I was born just before the Empress died, right before the beginning of King Mikal's reign and the outbreak of the Disease, which killed my parents and many others including the young princess and the Queen.

"How would you like to be dressed as a copy of me?" Grandmother asked, again holding up the dress for me to appreciate.

"I would hate it," I replied without hesitation.

"As would I," Grandmother agreed. "I am far more beautiful than you. I would feel great sorrow eclipsing your attention by my fair grace."

Invariably, that comment, which happened one or more times every Saturday, would cause me to erupt into laughter, while Grandmother did her best not to display her own mirth. Though Grandmother was probably only in her sixties, she was old to a girl my age, her skin wrinkled, her hair coarse and white, her hands freckled with spots.

I realized later, she was still quite beautiful for both her own age and any other, but to the child that was me, she simply could not compare to my youthful splendor.

"The Empress, the elder Sara, was more beautiful than the younger too. The little girl took after her grandfather, the Duke, and while a fine gentleman, and a genuinely kind man, His Royal Highness's looks were considerably lacking."

Grandmother's eyes grew misty as they did every time she thought of her youth.

"It was a different world then. So much hope, so much to look forward to. Ach, not at all like it is now."

Despite her distant thoughts, her fingers never once stopped their ministrations, nor ever lost a stitch, for she could sew with the same perfection with eyes closed.

"And, how did the little princess like the dress?" I asked. "Was it a success?" Having finished my tasked of hemming a skirt, I rose to take it to the iron.

"Let me see what you have done," Grandmother called sternly, not responding to my question. "Fine. Not your best work, but good enough for this lady. You'll be able to earn a coin or two from your skills if you keep it up. If you concentrate better, Ailana, you might even earn three or four. A good seamstress is always in demand by the nobility and rich."

"What nobility and rich?" I scoffed. "They are as poor as we are now."

"Anyone who has three coins to pay me is rich in my book," Grandmother snorted.

Turning on the steam, I carefully pressed out the skirt by placing it between two layers of special pressing cloth. As I stood there performing this laborious and boring task, I dreamed of future days in the university, surrounding myself with art and music, while discussing theories and philosophies with learned professors and brilliant students. We would sip dark espresso and think great thoughts, while planning how we would save our world and bring equality to all the races.

"That's all well and good, Ailana," Grandmother would say. "But, if you are not admitted into your fancy university, you best have a fallback plan to feed yourself."

I had no retort for this. I would be admitted of course. I was saving my money. I could earn a scholarship if I had to.

"It's not the money," Grandmother would cackle. "It never was. It's who you are and where your people are from. Heed my advice for I have seen it happen more times than I care to recall. It's the way of things. The pendulum swings both back and forth. Trust me. It is about to swing again."

"It's a new century," I replied. "We won't make the mistakes of your generation."

"It was a new century then, too, and we said the same."

"King Mikal has everything under control."

"He is a sad man, scarred by the Disease, and his own woes. The loss of his beloved wife and his little princess makes him long for the eternal rest. I fear our next king shall be his distant cousin, Duke Marko Korelesk and that does not bode well for our people, those who came from the motherland of Karupatani. Weak men always look for another to blame, and the Duke is both weak and dislikes our kind."

"I am not afraid," I replied smugly, placing the skirt upon a hanger, and covering it with a sheet of thin plastic wrap. "There is a movement afoot to elect a president instead of a king. We shall select someone smarter, someone caring who can represent us all. After Mikal, we shall be finished with the reign of kings and queens."

Grandmother hated it when I argued for democracy. Like her ire, the color rose in her face.

"People are stupid," she snapped, impatiently. "Too stupid to elect anyone who won't proclaim himself exactly that. Go on with you now, Miss University Girl. Go study your philosophy, but take a look at history too. When you are hungry, recall how to earn a coin by placing a stitch. It will feed you more than any art or music theories can provide."

"That will never happen," I retorted, already half way out her door.

"Of course it will. You just wait and see, for again it shall be us that are called to blame. Again, it shall be us who will become unwelcome in our homes. For this time, our motherland awaits. The Great Emperor granted it to us for all perpetuity. He knew two hundred years ago that this time would come to pass again."

I must have responded smartly. I always did. At the very least, I would have let the door slam shut behind me, as I hurried out, making an attempt to salvage the afternoon. I wouldn't let Grandmother's predictions bother me, for I heard the same every Saturday, and ignored them every time.

The motherland, the old ways held no attraction when the future beckoned. Frankly, only my grandmother belonged there, where they still practiced the Old Religion and kept the laws in those silly ancient books. To do this day, nearly two centuries since the Great Emperor had ended the wars and combined the races, only she still insisted we were of one and not the other.

But, I was the ignorant one, for time happened exactly as my grandmother foresaw. After King Mikal's death a dozen years into the future, while I was still a young mother, Grandmother's prophetic words unfortunately came true.

Chapter 4
Lance

My first year in the Allied SpaceForce aboard the Starship S/S Tornado was fairly uneventful if you consider spending six months of it in the sickbay stuck in a bed. I was waylaid fairly quickly by an attack of the space sickness which left most of my muscles unable to move. The only muscles that responded to any stimuli from my brain were those in my face, my heart and lungs, and the ones controlling my left pinkie finger. Unfortunately, while these muscles generally worked, there were times when even they simply chose to go to sleep, leaving me as productive as a zucchini on a stretcher.

"It's because of your previous nerve injuries," the ship's doc decided after studying the monitor above my head even though it always showed the same numbers and lines. "You were never fully recovered from that. You should have been screened out of space duty at your intake physical. You should have been assigned to guarding the fence at a landbase back on Earth."

I would have responded, if I could have. I would have told him about my galaxy-wide quest and shown him the ancient coin from the distant empire, but that moment was one of those times when my mouth randomly chose not to work. In fact, instead of talking I went into a coma-like state.

"Ah well, you're here now and we'll have to deal with it." The doc sighed, doing his best to return me to consciousness.

When I was alive again, but just barely, the doc summoned a nurse to my side.

"Nurse Moosy, this spaceman is your sole responsibility. Consider him your personal patient. See that he's well taken care of, and maybe, he'll survive so we can kick him out of SpaceForce."

Nurse Moosy nearly killed me, while at the same time, she was the only reason I was determined to make it through. This was because each morning, I awoke to the vision of her three, blue-skinned boobs hovering over my face.

She didn't do this on purpose, or so I thought. It was just the way she adjusted my meds, or took the readings from the monitor over my head. Each morning this alone caused my reluctant heart to jolt into action, which was followed only minutes later by a full cardiac arrest.

My heart wasn't the only organ that enjoyed her attention. When she changed my bedding or adjusted my catheter, other dormant parts of my body rose from the dead.

Nurse Moosy would giggle and blush, her pale blue face turning a shade of lavender with scattered lilac splotches, something I found incredibly attractive.

"Naughty spaceman," she'd say and waggle a finger in my direction.

"Mrr murf hamum," or something like that, I'd usually respond.

After several weeks in a nearly vegetative state, enjoying Nurse Moosy's attention from only inside my head, my body began to awaken and recover.

"Marry me," I declared to Nurse Moosy as she studied my blood pressure on the first morning when I could speak.

"Silly spaceman," she replied. "I don't know you well enough yet."

"You know every inch of my body and then some."

"I will go on a date when you are no longer my patient."

"Mrr murf hamum," or something like that, I mumbled, as she had stuck a probe in my mouth.

I reported back to duty and returned to my quarters, a tiny bunk in an even tinier cabin shared with three other guys. Borf was an enormous Andorian, who took up twice as much space as my other roommates, Wen and Noodnick. Noodnick definitely wasn't human, but what he was, I hadn't a clue, and frankly, wasn't too keen on finding out.

"You're back," Wen proclaimed, greeting me with a sort-of hug, even though I had met him only once before on the day I had come aboard. Wen had said he was human, and granted he looked like it, but there was something off about him, too, something that made me think he was also something else. "You are recovered, Lancelot?"

"It's just Lance, and yes, thanks for asking."

"Shut up!" Borf roared. "I'm trying to sleep."

Noodnick didn't say anything, which I guess was par for the course. According to Wen, the dude never spoke, or if he did, it wasn't audible to our ears.

My first day back on duty, I was assigned to a place we affectionately referred to as the engineering dungeon. There, I was given a console to monitor. Basically, I was to stand for eight hours and look at lights and gauges: oil pressure, water temperature, voltage, hydraulic pressure, engine temperature, hynautic pressure, and about forty other dials. If any one of them turned red, if a claxon sounded, or if I smelled smoke, I was to push another set of buttons and immediately inform the bridge.

"Why isn't this automated?" I asked my sergeant. "Don't we have a computer that can monitor this? Not that I'm complaining. I'll do my job. I was just wondering. You know…"

The guy glared at me and told me to shut up.

"It's because of the old Empire," Wen informed me later when he met me for a burger in the ship's cafeteria. "They used to supply the parts for our ships and since they're no more, our parts are no more, too. Now, we have to do everything the old fashion way." Wen giggled a little and gnawed his sandwich.

"I thought the old Empire was our enemy?" I opened the bun on my own sandwich and studied the meat, which tasted decidedly dull and looked decidedly weird. "Is this hamburger or what?"

"Synthetic," Wen replied. "I think it's pretty good." Taking another bite, while offering to eat mine, he told me how the old Empire was considered the Alliance's nemesis, but was also our biggest trading partner. "They sustained both of our economies."

"So, once they collapsed, they sent us back to the dark ages with them?" I asked.

"More or less," Wen nodded, looking vaguely like a squirrel, or a chipmunk, or some other type of rodent. "But, we are still flying and they are not. So, they are in the dark ages and we are only in about the 21st century."

"I'm not sure which was better. They were both pretty awful."

Wen laughed and finished my sandwich, enjoying it much more so than I ever would, while I picked at something that was supposedly a dill pickle.

The next day, I got up my nerve and decided to press Moosy for a date. She was in my thoughts from the simulated dawn to dusk, while her beautiful blue skin illuminated my dreams all night. During lunch, instead of eating with Wen again, I casually dropped by the sickbay to ask her out.

Unfortunately, Moosy was busy assisting the doc with some guy who had a heart problem. Even more unfortunate, when I asked if I could leave her a note, the other nurse took out an enormous hypodermic and informed me I was missing a few of the SpaceForce regulation shots.

After that, I left within a matter of seconds. Although both butt cheeks and arms were seriously in pain, that didn't stop me from running down the stairs back to my station. It was a good thing I did too, because just at that moment, the hydraulic system was glowing bright red. I arrived just in time to push my console buttons and sound the alarm, which set a bunch of other guys into action.

My quick thinking and quick button pushing pretty much saved the ship from disaster. Even more impressive, it got my sergeant to admit that I had done a good job. He recommended me for an award. I got a commendation, a nice plaque with my name and a picture of the ship, as well as a cash bonus, and a credit for two free dinners at the best little steakhouse chain in space.

"Hey, why don't I use it to take you out to dinner when we arrive at the spacebase tomorrow," I suggested to Moosy the following week.

I had taken to stalking the sickbay whenever she came off duty. I would wait for her to leave and then hand her a little cartoon I had drawn in my boredom.

"Marry me," I would scroll across the bottom of a picture of a rabbit proposing to a blue carrot, or two blue birds circling each other in flight, or once, a picture of a basket with two heads of blue lettuce.

At the time, I thought these were great ways to demonstrate my emotional state. Looking back later, I realized I was still recovering from a severe bout of space sickness. My brain had to have been severely traumatized to think that shit was romantic, or that my destiny was marriage to a woman from Andorus II.

"You are ill still," Wen had concluded, when he caught me doodling a pair of two blue snakes wound around and tied up in a love knot.

Moosy thought my notes were cute. Either that, or she was just being polite. She would reply with her sweet little giggle and a comment like, "Silly spaceman, you are so funny."

"Funny? Funny?!?" I'd cry aloud later in my cabin. "I'm in love and she thinks I'm joking. Oh my heart! How much can it take?"

"Shut up, asshole," Borf barked, showing me a fist the size of basketball. "Get back to sleep before I stuff you down the garbage chute and laugh as your head explodes in space."

I may have been foolishly in love, but fortunately, I was not a fool, or so I thought, when Moosy agreed to meet me at the steakhouse for lunch.

Spacebase 41-B was the largest base this side of the intergalactic divide, which made it a regular destination for Allied ships, both SpaceForce and commercial. The base had a thriving shopping mall and food court, as well as two hotels, theaters, and several bars.

On the lower levels, along with the docking bays, there was a large repair and storage facility. SpaceForce used this port of call to replenish our ship's stores and stock, as well as take care of any minor mechanical issues that might affect us before we headed into deep space. New crew were loaded, and old crew, whose contracts had expired, were free to debark. For some reason, those guys were always the first ones off the ship.

For the rest of us, unless your poor soul was specifically involved in the restocking process, or overseeing a repair, those forty-eight hours meant shore leave, a time so special, so wonderful, so liberating that it felt akin to a gift from the gods.

Walking off the Tornado with Wen that day, I was feeling pretty chipper. I had completely recovered from my space sickness, and had seven months of wages on my paycard, most of them earned while laying on my back. I was as wealthy as I had ever been, and I had a lunch date with a gorgeous woman, albeit one with blue skin and three boobs, which in my mind, made her all that much better. The only dark cloud spoiling the otherwise perfect view on my horizon, was the fact that I had to wear my spandex SpaceForce uniform to the restaurant. Due to weightloss during my illness, I didn't have any other clothes that still fit.

"So, where are we going?" Wen asked, bouncing along beside me, his squirrely face all lit up like a lightbulb.

"I am going to have lunch at the steakhouse with Moosy. I don't know what your plans are."

"I will hang out with you," he announced. "I have no other plans."

"Great," I mumbled, not wanting to hurt the guy's feelings, as frankly, other than Moosy, I had no friends aboard the starship either. "But, you're on your own for lunch. Let's go find a bank."

"Okay. I like banks," Wen declared. "I like all commerce. Commerce is the engine of our economy."

"Good Wen."

I never understood how a spacebase of that size, one that accommodated more than fifty thousand travelers coming and going on a daily basis, didn't have a bank in the mall. There were cash machines aplenty, none of which would do anything with my precious ancient Imperial coin other than spit it back out. There wasn't a real banker, or bank teller, or even android teller alive enough to look at it and tell me if I was unknowingly rich.

"Bummer," Wen said after we had checked ever shop and every kiosk on every floor of the base.

"I guess I'm stuck with it until the next base," I replied, pocketing it once again. "Maybe when we get closer to the old empire, someone will know what it's worth. Let's go into that Kwikie-Mart and see what they've got to eat."

"We can buy Kwikie food there," Wen cried joyfully. "Kwikie-sticks and Kwikie-chips, Kwikie-crunch and Kwikie chocolate cookies."

"Good, Wen," I said again, rounding the corner and entering the mini-mart's gates.

A bell sounded somewhere in the back as Wen immediately headed toward the junk food aisle. I was going to buy a box of chocolates, figuring Moosy might enjoy nuts and chews. While deciding between a two pound mixed assortment, or only dark caramels, the shop's bell dinged again and two sets of footfalls made their way across the floor. This was followed by what sounded like a happy squeal from the general direction of the cash register.

"Murmf bermuf yakwoof," or something like it, a woman cried, followed by the sounds of kissing, hugging and slapping on the back.

"A nice reunion." Wen sighed and pulled my arm. "Look Lancelot, Borf is with his wives."

"Uh huh," I murmured, snatching the dark caramels and the mixed nuts and chews off the shelf, before glancing up to see our roommate hugging two Andorian women at the register. "He's married to two?"

"Yep. And, he's got a husband, too," Wen informed me, as my heart ceased to beat and the world briefly spun and turned black. This was not because of the revelation about Borf's family situation, but rather the fact that I recognized Moosy tucked in the middle of her family's arms.

"He's her dad, right?"

"Nope. He's one of her husbands. Didn't you know that?"

Apparently not. I dropped both boxes of chocolates on the floor, before passing out right on top of them.

Needless to say, my romantic lunch date with Moosy was canceled. While Borf, or her other husband, Murf, who had been stocking the refrigerated case with sodas in the back of the Kwikie-Mart, didn't object to me taking her out, they all wanted to go. And, they all wanted to discuss my marriage proposal, for as I found out, marrying Moosy would mean I would also inherit all of them.

"Thanks for the steak," Wen declared later, wiping the last residue off his chin.

"No worries," I replied with a heavy sigh. "At least, I still have you."

Chapter 5
Jan

After those vehicles came and the shots sounded, I had no choice but to bring Dov home. I couldn't leave him on the street, huddling in doorways, or hiding in trash bins until they found him. Inevitably, they would. Our village was tiny and those trucks were filled with men.

My mother wouldn't take him in.

"A street orphan, Jan?" she cried. "You know what I think of this. If we bring one in and feed him, tomorrow there will be ten begging at our door. Go on, boy. Get you off my porch before anyone sees you here. Come back when you are alone, Jan." Mother slammed the door.

I looked at Dov, expecting his tiny face to be flooded with tears. Instead, he just shrugged, and smiled a little, his bright blue eyes impassive. Taking him next door to my Aunt Ailana's flat, I hoped there might be more compassion in my auntie's heart.

"No," Ailana snapped, refusing to open the screen. "Amyr is poorly today. I shan't let him be exposed to the street urchin's germs." Then, she too slammed the door in our faces, in the same manner as my mother. However, a moment later, it was cracked open just enough to pass a bowl of soup in Dov's direction. "Here. It's from Amyr. He wishes to share, although why, I cannot fathom. Let the boy drink it and be gone before your uncle, Pellen arrives home from his day at work."

"Thank you, Ma'am," Dov said politely and eagerly even though Auntie had once again slammed the door.

I watched Dov drink the soup, swallowing it quickly in great gulps as if he hadn't eaten in a week. It was kind of Amyr to share, but then again, my cousin always thought of every other before himself. When he was feeling poorly, as he did so often, he would make Auntie place his bowl outside to feed the people on the street.

"That was delicious." Dov sighed and with the back of his hand, he swiped at a trickle running down his chin.

It wasn't delicious, far from it actually, but to the starving child it could have been a meal fit for a king.

"I'll thank my cousin for you," I said, now taking the bowl back into Auntie's house.

Dov watched me, his eyes anxious and pleading, as if begging to follow me inside.

I was sorry I couldn't bring him in with me, for it would have been nice for him and Amyr to meet. Amyr would like him, I was certain. They might even become good friends. My cousin needed someone to play his games and keep him company, as no children came to visit except for me.

I didn't have any friends either, but that was purely by my choice. Mostly, I preferred the solitude of my boat, having little patience for anyone else in this tiny village. Amyr, on the other hand, professed interest in all who passed by his window.

"That's because you haven't met anybody bad," I told him. "Sitting here in your room, you meet only those who wish to see you, like doctors and nurses. Those sort of people are always nice.

"I have met the worst and more." He smiled mischievously and raised an eyebrow as if I might challenge his words.

"Amyr has lived quite a life in his imagination," Auntie Ailana replied.

I didn't think that was so terrible. In a way, it made up for the poor life he was living here in this flat.

Amyr was as close to me as a brother since we were cousins and had been raised side by side. In fact, in some ways, I cared more for him than my own brother, Taul. Despite being sickly and strange, there was also something about Amyr that made him sort of wonderful, although I couldn't say exactly what it was. Maybe, it was as simple as his imagination, something I lacked, or, maybe it was the joyful smile with which he greeted each day as if he was simply happy to be alive.

My mother said Amyr spoke as if he had the knowledge of many lifetimes in his soul, while my empty head indicated a soul that was completely new and blank. Daily, I attended school, filling my brain with language, science and math, while Amyr only ever left his house to visit the doctors. He wasn't strong enough to walk far, or even sit to hear a lesson. He didn't read either, for his odd eyes couldn't focus well enough upon a page. Yet, Amyr had knowledge of everything and would challenge me continuously with his thoughts, and I, four years older, would lose every debate.

Sometimes, I enjoyed his challenges. When he was feeling well, his humor was worth the mental exercise. Other times, my cousin's presence grew quite wearing. Then, I would tell him goodbye and return to the welcome solace of my boat, the sea, and the fish, who would accept me and my humble thoughts without an interrogation.

"I wish to sail on your boat someday," my cousin once said wistfully at my departure, filling me with remorse that I was leaving him again. "I would help you catch fish to sell. I would like to be upon the sea."

"Perhaps, you will," I replied. "When you are strong and healthy."

He smiled and laughed a little, for he had never been either of those things.

"I might as well wish to grow wings and fly high above, upon the currents of air."

"Tsk tsk," my auntie would cluck, shaking her head and rolling her eyes. "What sort of son do I have that cannot walk, but dreams of flying like a bird?"

My mother fretted a little about my reticence to socialize with anyone other than Amyr. She was afraid I would never find a man to marry, and thus, would depend on her throughout my life. I saw no issue with this. I was content in our village and our tiny home, fully satisfied with only her presence for my company.

In fact, when my brother, Taul returned from wherever he had gone, I felt his arrival as an unwelcome disruption to our routine. Our tiny house seemed only tinier with him spread upon the couch. My mother's doting upon my brother, especially as his appearances became fewer and further between, bothered me like a tiny fish bone stuck in my throat.

During those days, I would spend more time out on my boat on the pretense we needed more fish to quench my brother's appetite. If the weather did not cooperate, I would visit Amyr for long hours, even sleeping upon the floor next to his sofa or chair. I was always relieved when my brother set out again to wherever he chose to go and the pattern of my home returned to normal.

"The Korelesk army has come to the western border of the mountains," Taul said, only weeks before the day that I met Dov. "It won't be long until they are here at our doorstep. I've heard terrible things about the army and what they do to people like us."

"Don't speak such nonsense. Those are only rumors meant to cause us fear." My mother served Taul a portion of fish from the pot of soup on top the stove. I liked this recipe very much. It was one from the motherland, handed down from her grandmother before. "Everything is fine, Jan. Eat your fish and then take a portion next door to your cousin. Ailana says he fares poorly and this soup will give him strength."

"I want to hear about the Duke of Korelesk," I protested, reluctantly rising from my seat to prepare a bowl for Amyr.

"I have nothing more to say," Taul replied, sharing a knowing look with Mother. Obviously, there was more, but they didn't want me to hear.

Amyr had been sleeping when I knocked upon his door, so I returned to my own table a few moments later, having left the soup with Aunt Ailana to eat herself. Taul was speaking in hushed tones, while my mother's face had gone even paler than before.

"The other dukes have small armies, if they have an army at all. None can compete with Korelesk's strength if he tries to take the crown."

"We may have to return to the motherland," my mother murmured fretfully. "We won't be safe anywhere else."

"I'd rather go to outer space," Taul declared. "I will join a merchant ship, and fly far away to a distant star. Then, I will send for you."

"Not I. I have no desire to go. Better you should send the aliens to stop Korelesk before he kills us all."

"What about you, Jan?" My brother turned to me.

In the meantime, my mother rose, her eyes panning across my face. Would I fly away to another world with Taul, or would I return to the motherland, a distant continent across the sea?

"I don't want to go to outer space either," I declared, imagining a world of endless nights. It would be cold and frightening out there, flying through the darkness to distant stars. Perhaps, it was even filled with strange alien beings who might enslave us and treat us worse than the Duke of Korelesk. "I would rather go to the motherland. I've heard it is green and fruitful, and the waters are always filled with fish."

"Where did you hear that?" Mother asked, now setting Taul's dessert before him. It was a handful of berries diligently gathered from the forest.

"Amyr said so."

Watching Taul eat his berries, I wished I could have a few. There weren't enough though, as it was still too early in the spring. Only Taul got such a prize because his visits were so few, but next time, when he was far across the stars, all the berries would be for me.

"Amyr." Taul sniffed and shook his head a little, rolling his eyes, while sharing a knowing glance with Mother. "What else does our fanciful cousin say of this land he has never been to, nor couldn't see if he had?"

"Nothing," I murmured. "Nothing else at all."

In truth, Amyr had told me much of our peoples' former home, describing it as if he had lived there long ago.

"You shall like it there, Jan," he had told me. "There you shall find a man to love you, a man like you."

I believed him, for Amyr only spoke the truth.

Taul left the next day, and as usual when he departed, my mother wept for an entire week.

"Where do you think he will go?" I asked Amyr, arriving at his side with a fresh bowl of fish soup. "Will he come back or will he die in outer space?"

Amyr frowned and supped the broth. I could tell he was feeling better this day, as he was sitting upright, and there was a slight pinkness to his normally wan cheeks. Like me, his skin was pale, but unlike me, his hair was as black as night, making an interesting contrast that seemed to give pause to all who met him. Today, his hair glowed as if the sun was shining singularly upon him, and his eyes were filled with colors, although I couldn't say which ones.

"He won't die in outer space," my cousin replied thoughtfully, a small smile tugging at his lips. "Do not fear for it shan't be the last time you see your brother. He is doing what he is called to do."

I nodded. I liked when Amyr spoke as if the future was written and displayed before his eyes. He always smiled when he did this, which made me think the future wouldn't be so bad.

"What am I called to do?"

"Play chess with me," Amyr declared, reaching for the ancient marble set stored on a tray beneath his chair. Uncle had carried it home one day, saying it was brought to him by a man who claimed to have received it from the Duke of Turko.

"He said it once belonged to the Great Emperor," Uncle had cried excitedly. "See here the Imperial Signet stamped upon the bottom of each piece."

"Can you see it, Amyr?" I had asked, holding the white queen close to his strange eyes.

"I see it." Amyr smiled, but I didn't believe him because his eyes were closed.

"Aw," I moaned then as he began to set up the board, for I was none too pleased to be invited to play this game. Although given the choice of returning to my weeping mother or remaining here, my options were both poor. "Alright, but where is the black king and white queen? We are missing two very important pieces, cousin."

"I gave them to Taul before he left. We can use salt and pepper shakers instead."

"Amyr," my aunt interrupted, fortunately for me. "Jan isn't here to entertain you. She has fish to catch. Work to do. Unlike you, Jan has no free time."

Auntie was working a fine cloth, something shiny and satiny that belonged to a rich lady. It rustled between her fingers and reflected light across the room. I imagined a dress made of this material, briefly envisioning how it might appear on me, before brushing that thought aside. That was something I would never wear.

"And, I have nothing but free time," Amyr agreed. "Endless hours to sit and think. But, it is raining and Jan doesn't like fishing in the rain. Furthermore, the wind will come up to ruin her sail and rock her boat. Go get the shakers, Jan. I'm setting the board so you will be white."

"It's not raining," I said, nodding toward the window where long, dirty streaks made the blue sky look as if it was dark and gray. "But, Auntie is right. I am busy."

In truth, I hated playing chess with Amyr. Despite my best efforts, he always won. Occasionally, he would let me get close by capturing a rook, a knight, and several pawns. Once or twice, he even let me capture his queen, giving me false hope, making me believe that I might survive. Then, in a blink of an eye, he had my king locked in a deadly trap.

Amyr smiled and shrugged a little, just as thunder clapped overhead. Giant splatters of rain pinged against the filthy window.

"You see? It is a poor day to be out in a boat."

"I promised my mother I would clean the house. She has taken to her bed in sorrow over Taul's departure. I'm sorry, Amyr. Perhaps, we can play another time?"

"Perhaps." He yawned and closed his eyes, absolving my guilty conscience for he was tired.

"Embo is acting ridiculous," Aunt Ailana declared. "Your mother's theatrics are exactly that. But, go on, Jan. Amyr doesn't need you. He can play chess against himself just as well. It's a pity his eyesight is too poor to stitch, else he could sit here and earn a coin the same as me."

"Now, you know why my eyesight is poor," my cousin teased lightly, in between another yawn. His eyes closed, and his long dark lashes created a fan across his cheek. "When the angels asked if I should like to see, but in exchange I must stitch and sew, I promptly refused their generous offer, and chose to be helpless instead."

"Oh Amyr," my auntie sighed, "what will I do with you?"

"You will kill me," he joked as I shut the door.

Now, weeks later, I found myself again outside their door with the little street urchin, Dov, who had nowhere to go.

"That soup was really delicious. Do you think they might give me some more?"

I shook my head. Both Mother and Auntie would blame me for encouraging him.

"I'm sorry."

He shrugged again. "That's okay. Thanks for sharing it with me."

"Thank my cousin if you ever get to meet him. You should hide beneath our porch, or behind that large shrub next to the house. If the Korelesk army comes, they probably won't look over there."

Dov shook his head and jumped off the porch, landing on both feet. He smiled as if that was great fun.

"Goodbye Jan." He skipped to the street, and were it not for the wind, I would have heard him singing a silly, childish song, his torn, sleeveless shirt bouncing up and down, dancing in the rain.

Chapter 6
Pellen

"They say there is fighting in the streets, Papa. Did you see it?" Amyr called to me as soon as I opened the door.

I was tired and my back aching from far too many hours of standing on the cement floor. My heart, too, was aching from far too many hours of standing with only a few coins to show for my efforts. Three coins were not enough to feed my wife and myself, let alone the boy whose medicine cost twice as much each week.

"No." I spoke truthfully for my journey home had been uneventful.

However, there had been whispers on the street, although I tried not to listen. Purposefully, I had walked with my head down and my eyes unfocused, so as not to call attention to myself. Yet, I heard wisps of strangers' conversations unmistakable in their meaning. Everyone was speaking the same. The same words were repeated from corner to corner, doorstep to doorstep. Evil had come to us and no longer were we safe.

"Are you certain?" my son asked. "I thought I heard the sounds of guns."

"Hush," Ailana snapped, putting her hand on the boy. "It was only your imagination, or the thunder in the hills. I heard nothing. There is no reason to worry. Don't overly excite yourself, child. Sit back down and calm your heart."

"Are you sure you didn't see anything, Papa?" the child persisted as I lay down upon the floor.

I was too worn even to remove my boots, as my heart was now beating double time worrying after his. Would that I could give my son my own strong organ in exchange for the one that beat so weak. If not, would that I could take this child away from this poor, sad village where he could not be cured.

"I saw nothing." I forced a smile into my voice, while keeping it calm and low, lest the child or my wife hear my fear. "I saw only the jagged cracks in the pavement. If I did not watch for them, I might have fallen through, and ended up in the motherland on the other side of the planet."

Amyr laughed, but Ailana only rolled her eyes.

"Take off your coat, Pellen. You are dripping water on the floor."

"Jan saw something," Amyr reported as I hung my coat upon its peg. "She said they made a tremendous noise." This filled my son with excitement, for he began to bounce as he lay upon the worn couch.

"Hush Amyr," my wife said again, for the boy's exertion might lead to a fit. Sometimes, the medicines helped to control the spasms, while other times, we could do nothing but stand helplessly and watch.

"Your niece has a tendency to exaggerate," I reminded Ailana. "The trucks might have merely been provisions from the government."

"No." Amyr held himself upright to look at me.

I turned to face my boy, never failing to appreciate the beauty of his appearance. Where and from whom his unique looks descended, I could only guess. Certainly, it wasn't me, for my hair was a plain, ordinary brown, my nose overly large, and my dark eyes too closely set.

While I appreciated Ailana's looks, she, too, paled in comparison to the boy. Neither was her golden beauty passed on to him. Instead, he eclipsed her with his shiny black hair, pale skin as fine as porcelain, and eyes that could only be described as singularly unique.

On cold winter days, Amyr's eyes echoed the snow. When thunder raged overhead, they were as dark and foreboding as the rain. During the spring, they glistened with color, and in the summer, they shone as golden as the sun. On the rare occasions when he grew angry, they flamed as if filled with fire burning red. Yet, for such unique and exceptionally beautiful organs, they were surprisingly poor when it came to performing their task.

My son was born sickly. Since his arrival, several months earlier than he should have appeared, his growth had been marred by the advancement of his poor condition.

"We haven't the facilities to treat him anymore," the doctor had said, shortly after his birth. "Years ago, during the reign of the Empress Sara, we could have helped him. Now, I can only give you a medicine to alleviate his pain."

"What will become of him?" Ailana had gasped, clutching the baby to her chest, fearing the loss of someone we had only just come to know.

The doctor didn't respond. My son's list of ailments was far too long to recite. Her time was better spent with patients, some whom might not only pay her, but be cured.

Amyr was still alive now, and every day was a joy and a reason to give thanks. He was an exceptionally bright and cheerful child, his wit as sharp as his intelligence was cunning. But, he was weak and so each day ended with the fear that this one might be his last. Tonight, his heart might cease to beat. If not, tomorrow, his brain might seize and grow silent.

I loved the child with everything that was within me and would have given him my healthy body in an instant if I could. Yet, there were nights when I wished for it all to be done, to wake up and discover this nightmare had finally ended. I told myself he would be at peace.

In the mornings, I would chastise myself and fall prostrate upon the floor in prayer. I would expunge those evil thoughts from my soul, for God had given me this child for a reason. Although my son's purpose amongst us was not apparent now, I knew that someday I would understand it all, and so I went about my daily tasks with my son forever on the tip of my mind.

Foregoing breakfast, I would depart early to walk to my shop, whereupon I would stand for twelve hours on the cement. My aching back and my worn heart were just penance for the evil thoughts about someone who I so dearly loved.

Again, the next night, in the darkest and coldest hours, when the last of the heat had gone from the hearth, those black thoughts would creep into my mind. How many coins would we have without his medicine? What food could I give to Ailana, who like her cousin was now as slim as stick? Without this child and his burdens, might we leave this place and return to the motherland, for it was only Amyr and his medicines who kept us here.

"Jan brought a child home with her," Ailana said, removing the worn boots from my feet, which briefly celebrated the joy of being set free. I moved closer to the fire, letting the flames warm my toes and soles, as Ailana headed to the kitchen to fetch a needle and thread. Her skirts swished behind her, hanging loosely from her thin frame. If I looked closely, I would see bones jutting from beneath her blouse. "I see you have another hole in the left one." Her voice scolded wearily. "I should repair it now while the leather is still wet and supple."

"Don't. Leave it be." Her fingers would be sore and blistered, aching more so than my back and feet, for she spent the same hours stitching in exchange for a coin or a cup of flour. "Another day, I can manage. Another week, I can walk. There is no hurry, Ailana. Come sit by the fire and warm yourself with me."

"Don't tell me what to do," she snapped, returning with both her sewing implements and a cup of lukewarm broth. A tiny cloud of fat floated at the top. A single dumpling of dough formed like a lump in the very center.

"Amyr, have you supped?" I asked, offering my cup firstly to the boy.

My son shook his head.

"I'm not hungry, Papa. I gave my cup to Jan for her friend. He needed it more than I. He was very hungry."

"A waste," Ailana spat, her hands already busily filling my boot's hole. "Feeding a child off the street when we haven't enough to fill our own bellies."

I glanced back at my son, while drinking my broth with relish. Despite its weak contents, it tasted it good, especially since this day, I had eaten only a single egg and a crust of hard bread. Amyr was smiling, his odd eyes shining with color, reflecting the flames in the hearth despite the darkness surrounding him.

Ailana sniffed loudly and shrugged a cold shoulder in Amyr's direction. "A little boy," she muttered under breath.

"A little boy," I echoed with a chuckle. "Tell me about your friend, my son. Did Mama let you invite him in?"

Setting my empty cup down on the floor beside me, I lay flat, the only position comfortable for my back, and stared at the vein like cracks crisscrossing the ceiling. Were they getting worse? Wasn't that large one down the center a little less only yesterday? Someday, this ceiling would collapse upon us and I would be powerless to put it back. Someday the world would collapse around us, and I, Shopkeeper Pellen would be powerless to provide for my family.

"Jan found him by the boat. Then, the trucks came and shot up everything on the street. Jan and her friend ran home as fast as they could, but neither Mama nor Aunt Embo wouldn't let the boy come in their house."

"Calm down, Amyr!" Ailana cried. "That's enough of this tale. If we let every lost child inside, there would be no space or food for you."

My wife was correct, as unfortunate as it was. There were more lost children on the street than we could ever feed. My heart broke as I passed them, begging, stealing, or too weak to even try. That was the way of it now, not only in our village, but throughout the land. Who could help them? Not I. I had not enough bread to feed my own sickly son.

"We should go to the motherland," I whispered to Ailana later that night as the two of us huddled beneath our blanket. Neither of us slept, but instead we both listened for the steady sound of Amyr's breath.

In and out, he gasped, occasionally marked by a cough, or an unintelligible murmuring that almost sounded like another tongue.

"There are no medicines there," my wife scoffed, repeating what we both knew. "Wishes and prayers, smoke and incense, dances and songs will not stave off the spells or keep his heart beating."

"If the army has come for us, the hospital will refuse us entrance. The doctors will act as if we are not there. No longer will they give us the medicines that he needs."

"We don't even speak the language, Pellen. We have no memories, no ties to that place."

"It is in our blood and in our souls," I insisted. "We can learn to speak and grow our roots again, just as our grandparents did when they came here. If the army has truly come, if it is as the whisperings suggest, the motherland is the only place where we will be safe."

My wife said nothing more, for she knew that I spoke the truth, yet she would not admit to it, nor even consider my request. She turned her back to me and soon, I could hear the steady rhythm of her slumbers intertwined with Amyr's breathing in and out.

Chapter 7
Ailana

Amyr had a spell just before morning. I heard him choking and thrashing in the depths of my sleep. Even if I hadn't heard him, I would have awaken. I always knew when he was suffering. It was almost as if an alarm would begin to sound deep within my soul.

"What is it?" Pellen mumbled, reaching for me as I stirred. The foolish man thought it was because of him that I had awakened, that I might want him now in the light of the early dawn.

"Amyr," I cried, slapping at my husband's arms and rushing across the room to my child.

He had gone still. If he was breathing, I couldn't hear it. Laying my head upon his chest, I searched for the sound of his heart, willing for it to beat, begging it to stir.

"Amyr!" Pellen yelled, now rushing to my side, trying to awaken the boy with the sound of his voice. "Amyr!"

Pellen reached in the boy's mouth, lest his tongue again be blocking his throat. Then, he slapped at my child's face and his chest.

My son coughed, his cheek red with the imprint of Pellen's hand. His eyelids rolled back and in the dim light of the dawn, the boy's eyes swirled with a thousand different colors.

Amyr jolted a little, as if his heart had suddenly tripped again. He gasped, before heaving a long, heavy sigh.

"I'm alright, Mama," he whispered wearily, closing his brilliant eyes to this world. "I am here with you now. I am back again."

"My child," I wept, now pulling his head to my breast, willing him to breathe, to live, and to grow. Would that he was still inside me, safe and protected in my womb, instead of in this harsh world in a body that fought to stay.

"We have to do something," Pellen declared angrily, as if there was a remedy we hadn't tried. "We have to find a doctor who will help. There must be some kind of cure. In the motherland…"

"No!" I shouted, causing Amyr's eyes to fly open once again. "I will not go there. I will not take him across the ocean to certain death."

Pellen turned away. He went back to our blankets by the fire, which was only a small cluster of orange embers in the center of the hearth. He lay down and feigned sleep, although I knew he remained awake. His breathing was too strong, too determined, too filled with hate.

"Go back to sleep, Mama." Amyr pushed himself from me. Rolling over, his voice became muffled by his pillow. "There is nothing more which you can do tonight. Leave me be. I am so tired."

I abandoned my son to his wishes and returned to my husband's side, my own heart filled with both grief and hate. I hated this life. I hated the cold morning air and the fire that was too weak to warm me. I hated the dawn for it meant that soon I would have to arise and once again, pick up my needles and thread.

I hated my husband for his sad face, his bent back, his cowed demeanor, and most of all, his inability to heal my son and fix the wrongs in our tiny world.

And, I hated my son. I hated his sickness, and the way his every breath controlled the beatings of my heart. I hated myself at the same time, for what mother would ever wish her child dead, especially when the child was so beautiful, so kind, and so extraordinarily good?

"Ailana," my cousin called, storming into my room that next morning, a fine man's coat tossed over her arm. "The gentleman wants this today, and I have far too many others to do."

"And, you think I don't?" I picked up a dress from my bundle and shook it in her direction.

"Please Ailana!" Embo tossed the coat at me. It landed on the floor at my feet, kicking up a cloud of dust, lint, and stray threads before settling in a puddle. "Clean that before you return it to me." She turned on heel and slammed the front door.

"Kari-fa! How I hate the woman!" I swore, kicking the coat, which I most certainly would not do.

I wouldn't touch it. All morning I sewed the items in my basket, in between tending the fire, and seeing to the house. My child was fast asleep. Often when his night was so difficult, he would sleep all through one day and into the next, while I had no choice but to toil despite my fatigue.

Pellen would return hungry from his shop and I had nothing to give him. Barely a cup was left of the bone soup, certainly not enough to feed three. My bread box was similarly empty with only a hard heel of black bread and a few crumbs of something green with mold.

Pellen would eat it. He'd scrape off the mold and toast whatever remained over the fire, while giving the black bread heel to Amyr, who would savor it as if it was a delicacy.

"Have some, Mama," my good child would say, breaking the tiny piece in two. My sickly angel would share the last crumb even if it meant he would die instead.

I would shake my head. "You need it more than I." And, I would eat nothing, for I was healthy despite my lack of food.

Embo might bring me a bit of dried fish later, in exchange for mending her gentleman's coat. I might find a spare root in between my garden weeds, with which I could turn the two of them into a soup. The hunger never bothered me anymore. In fact, the memory alone of the large banquets at my grandmother's table would turn my stomach inside out, or roil it with bile.

Instead, I pushed those images from my mind and concentrated on my sewing, while listening for the steady intake of my child's breath. In and out. In and out. He slept peacefully until the gunshots sounded in the distance. Heavy booms rocked the house as if thunder was directly overhead even though the day was clear and the sky empty, save a single forlorn cloud.

My front door swung open, causing me to shriek with fright, but it was only Jan come running from next door.

"They're here!" my niece gasped breathlessly. "The neighbor says it is the Duke's army come to take us from our village and enslave us in their work camps. We need to hide!"

"Hide where? Hide how? How do you know this, child?" I tossed the sewing aside, glancing at Amyr, whose eyes were still heavily closed.

"Everyone is running to the forest!" Jan jumped up and down like a petulant child, while the sounds of more guns echoed across the street. "Mama is packing us a bag. You best do it too. Five minutes, Mama says, and we must be gone."

A bag of what? I had nothing worth keeping other than the rags on my back, or this gentleman's coat which I could wrap around Amyr. But, how could I carry him to the forest, and what of my husband? If the Duke's army was truly here, Pellen might already be dead.

"I can carry Amyr," Jan offered, answering the question before it left my lips. "I have to hurry now to help Mama, but I'll return and hoist him upon my back."

The door slammed again and still Amyr didn't stir. Someone screamed in the alley, and I froze. I couldn't run away to hide in the forest among the trees. I had lived like this once before, vowing never again to sleep where there was no roof above my head.

Grandmother's voice spoke, although only I could hear her in the back of my brain.

"You are strong, Ailana. You are like me. You will fight and you will survive no matter the cost."

"What of my son, Grandmother?" I asked.

Amyr coughed then, interrupting my silent conversation. At the same time, the fire crackled, a flame suddenly shooting upward, sending light and heat across the room.

I tamped it down and rose to my feet, standing over Amyr on the couch. What of this child, this useless, sickly boy who was too weak to walk?

If we stayed and the army came, surely they would kill him first. However, if I took him to the forest, his presence would weigh the others down. We'd have to carry him everywhere. He might have a spell and call out when we must be quiet. He might kill us all simply by trying to save his life.

My son, my love, my heart was a burden and not worth the price of a village full of souls. Despite his beauty and his wit, he would never be what he had been intended.

I could do him a favor and all of us, if I took his life now, here on the couch while he slept unaware. He would pass from this mad world and this bad time to a better place.

I told myself this. I rationalized the murder of my beloved child, knowing full and well that I would have to live forever with this choice. But, would I rather see him slain by a gunshot, or waste away only to be eaten by the forest creatures? No. I would kill him now. I, who gave him life, would take it back.

He stirred just then, his brilliant eyes flickering open as if he had heard my thoughts. He stared at me, all the colors of the rainbow shining upon my face.

"I have no choice," I wept, clutching the pillow with which I meant to quell his breath. "Go quietly, my love. Don't make this more difficult than it is."

I pressed the pillow upon his face and with all my strength I held it fast. He was weak, his muscles small and unused. I did not expect him to fight me. I thought he would go limp and his chest to rattle with a final gasp. I did not expect my husband to race through the door and pull me away.

"What are you doing, Ailana?" Pellen tossed me on the floor with a strength I never knew he had.

"Leave him! Let him die! Pellen, please."

Pellen hastened to pull the boy upright and slapped at his face, bidding the child to wake again and breathe. Amyr made a noise, a small intake of breath, a moan and once again, a bright flame shot upward from the hearth.

"No! Let him go!" I wept, although I knew not why. What sort of mother was I that begged for my own beloved child's death?

Jan called to us just then, bidding us to hurry before the army arrived on our street. As if in a dream, I watched my husband carry my son to the door.

"Are you coming?" he demanded. "Get yourself up, Ailana. Let's go."

I couldn't. I wouldn't. My legs refused to stand.

"Fine. You stay. After what you have done to Amyr, you deserve to die."

"He would be better off dead!" I shouted. "All of us would be better off if he was dead. Admit it, Pellen. You have thought the same yourself."

"He's our son. I will protect him with my life even if it means I shall draw my last breath."

"You will," I declared with a foresight I didn't know I had. "You don't know who he is. You don't know why he lives, or why he is here again."

This stopped Pellen in his tracks. Despite his haste to depart, he turned to me and demanded to know what I had meant.

"Have you gone insane, Ailana? Of course, I know who is. He is our beloved son, conceived in marriage, conceived in love."

"No, you're wrong," I announced before Pellen slammed shut the door. "He was never conceived in love and neither was he ever your son."

Chapter 8
Jan

"Where is Ailana?" my mother called to Pellen as he lifted Amyr through the hole in the fence. I was already waiting on the other side to catch him.

"She is not coming."

"What?" my mother gasped, as I gazed at the others who crouched alongside the wall. Some were already sidling around the corner, or crawling through the bent path of overgrown grass. I was anxious to follow them, to run with them to the freedom that awaited, to begin an adventure outside our village and the only world I had known.

Instead, I held out my arms for Amyr, hefting him upon my back, wrapping his legs around my waist, softly snorting and pawing the ground as if I was his horse. I had carried him like this before. His weight was not more than a basket of fish on a day that I had done well, and certainly, he was easier to carry and less smelly.

"Hold tightly, cousin," I called loping along after the crowd. "We're going exploring in the woods. You are a great hunter and a brave warrior of our people, while I am your trusty and swift-footed steed."

"Doesn't she understand what will happen if she stays?" my mother called to Uncle as he began to follow me. "Go back and fetch her. Implore her not to be a fool."

"I have already done so, but she is out of her head," Pellen replied, prompting my mother to climb back through the fence herself. "You won't be able to convince her, Embo. Save yourself. Don't worry after her. I will use my energy to save my son. Give him to me, Jan. He is too heavy for you to carry long." Coming up beside me, Uncle removed Amyr from my back.

Suddenly alone, I hesitated, undecided if I should return to assist my mother and Auntie.

"Stay here, Jan," Uncle said, just as the bushes rustled beside me.

"Hi!" that street boy, Dov called, a large grin spread across his face. "Are you coming?" He held out his hand.

"To where?" I looked back at the hole in the fence.

"The hideout, of course. This will be fun!"

"Jan," Uncle called again, just as loud voices began to shout. Their calls echoed off the buildings and were accompanied by that now familiar sound of heavy trucks.

"Let's go," Dov cried, reaching for my hand. Though he was small, he was surprisingly strong as he pulled me into the woods, following Uncle and Amyr.

"What of my mother? What of Auntie?"

"Too late," the boy said. "There is nothing to be done."

Although, my knees were weak and my feet stumbled on nearly every step. I let the child lead me as my mind went numb. How long our journey took, or how far we traveled beneath the canopy of the trees, I couldn't begin to recount. All I knew was at the end, I fell into the safety of Pellen's arms, surrounded by a few others from our village.

It was already dark then, and cold, for no one would light a fire, lest it attract the army's attention. Instead, throughout that first night, we huddled together in small groups, sheltered behind fallen logs and large tree trunks, or buried beneath moss and brush.

It was not an adventure as I had hoped, but a long cold night in a dark hellish place. Every sound sent a spike of fear down my spine even if it was only the scampering of a squirrel across the limbs above us, or the whisper of a night owl's wings.

Sometime during the darkness, we heard the sound of footsteps trampling about the woods and the whispering of men's voices as they passed by. Brush rustled as it was pushed aside and beams of light illuminated the trees above our heads. I didn't breathe until they disappeared, and I didn't move a muscle no matter how my limbs ached.

I clutched tightly to Dov as if he was my own brother, for now, like him I was orphaned and alone. Next to me, Pellen held Amyr upon his lap, my cousin's head laying tightly against his father's chest.

"Don't be afraid," my uncle murmured. "I will always protect you."

"I am not afraid," Amyr whispered softly, his eyes hard and cold like the dark forest. "They can do nothing to me that hasn't been done."

"We're safe with Amyr," Dov whispered beside me. "He'll protect us."

Amyr? Protect us? My weak and sickly cousin?

The street boy smiled and clasped my hand. "He always does."

In the morning, some wanted to walk again, while others thought it better if we remained hidden where we were.

"Duke Korelesk's army won't stay in the village forever," a woman assured us. "They'll depart after they have looted our things."

"We need to walk westward," a man disagreed. "It is not far to the ocean and from there we can build a boat. The motherland will welcome us. This country doesn't want us anymore."

"We'll die in the transit," a third declared. "Who here can walk all the way to the ocean? We are already nothing more than skin and bones from lack of food. And, if we were to get there, who here can build a boat to cross it? We haven't a stick of wood or a nail to fasten it together. The ocean is enormous, the water a cruel master, and the wind, his mistress."

"We have no choice," my uncle Pellen interrupted. "The motherland is the only place where we will be safe."

"I have a boat," I almost announced, but Dov tugged my hand sharply and bid me to be quiet.

"Your boat won't fit everyone here," he hissed. "It will only be enough for you and I, your uncle and cousin."

"My mother and Auntie?"

Dov shook his head. "The Duke's army has taken them away. That's what they do in every village. Or, they kill them." His voice went soft, as if he wished to bite back the words, to save me from their meaning.

"Is that what happened to your parents?"

"Mhm. But, I came here." He squeezed my hand again as if to show he had done this all for me.

Pellen and the other adults argued back and forth while the sun rose above the treetops. Odd rays of light shone down through the forest, illuminating the brush like a torch from another world.

The light almost seemed to make a staircase to the outer space where my brother lived. I imagined Taul stepping into those golden beams and magically, rising upward to the stars. From there, he would board a ship that would take him to a warm and happy planet. Or, he might live there on that ship, sailing from star to star as I dreamed of sailing upon the sea, both of us searching for a place we would be safe.

"Jan," Pellen whispered while the other villagers continued to argue. "Where is your boat now? Do you think we can sneak over to it tonight?"

I turned to my uncle, to tell him I thought so, when instead, my eyes were drawn to my cousin's face. Amyr had his chin tipped upward and his eyes were open as if he was staring at the sun. Their color was as silver as the rays, echoing the light which seemed to circle about his body like a shimmering aura.

"Amyr!" I gasped. "What has happened to you?"

Amyr blinked and the aura instantly disappeared, making me doubt that it had ever been there.

"It's not far from here, is it, Jan?" Pellen continued, obviously not having seen the light surrounding his son. "Do you think you can find the wharf in the dark?"

"I can find it," Dov declared. "And, I can help to sail the boat."

"Then, it is decided." Pellen set Amyr down beside Dov, slowly rising to his feet. His knees creaked as he leaned forward, reaching with a hand to rub the small of his back. "I am unused to sitting all night upon the forest floor." He smiled apologetically, although no one faulted him for ailing in this way. "I shall go find something for you children to eat. Jan, I know you want to come hunting, but I would prefer you stayed here to look after the boys."

"Yes, Uncle." I didn't mind staying as I was tired from lack of sleep, during a night filled with fear and freezing temperatures. Thoughts of my mother and Auntie swarmed at the back of my mind threatening my resolve not to break down in tears.

"Keep quiet and well hidden. I shall be back as soon as I can."

I watched as Pellen disappeared among the trees, wondering if he too would not return.

"We could go by ourselves," Dov whispered. "If we had to, I mean."

"He'll return," Amyr replied with his knowing certainty.

Despite our desperate circumstances, my cousin had awoken this day in better health. There was faint color in his cheeks and he was sitting up unaided. His odd eyes reflected a spectrum of green shades like the forest and his wavy black hair seemed to shine with the remnants of that strange aura.

I wanted to ask him of our mothers, but took his silence as the response. Surely, if they would join us, he would have announced this before. Instead, I began to plan our journey, our trek to the river and our voyage to the sea, hoping the wind and tides would take us where we needed to go.

"If the wind is kind to us, I think we should arrive in the motherland in less than a week."

"I agree," Dov said. "The winds will push us all the way there. Maybe, a giant wave will come and we will ride it like a great, galloping horse."

"What do you think, Amyr? What does the future tell of our voyage?" I looked again to my cousin, whose opinion I trusted above all.

Amyr closed his eyes. He yawned and stretched, his fists balled.

"The winds will be kind," he said after a bit. "But, the sea is always cruel. We have no choice, though. If we stay here, we will surely die."

We ate a handful of wild berries, tiny blue ones that would have been better if they ripened another week. Pellen apologized as if it was his fault we were without food. Lifting Amyr into his arms, he bid us follow the other villagers further into the woodlands.

Although they tried to keep their voices low, our neighbors argued incessantly. If any of the Korelesk army had been about, surely they would have found us by the loud hissing of their voices.

Eventually, before nightfall, a shouting match ensued, whereupon our group broke into two camps. Those that wanted to walk to the sea, and those that wanted to turn and fight, decided they were better off without each other.

It was then that we ducked away.

"They won't notice us now," Pellen hissed, pulling my arm. In turn, I grabbed Dov's hand and we scrambled into the brush, our neighbors argument following us for quite a distance.

We walked slowly since it was already dusk and we were exhausted after a sleepless night, as well as a day spent stumbling over branches and logs with little food in our bellies. My arms and legs were scratched in a million places and where they weren't, mosquitos had sought to bite. But, as bad a condition as I was in, poor Pellen looked as if he would soon collapse.

"Let me carry Amyr for a while," I offered, but Pellen refused, shifting my cousin onto his back. Amyr's head lay upon his father's shoulder, but his eyes were open as if watching all we passed. Every once in a while, they seemed to flicker, a tiny flame igniting deep inside. Every once in a while, he would lift his head and smile, prompting Dov to giggle as if the two shared a secret.

We emerged from the forest up river of the village when the mother moon was still chasing the child moon from the early morning sky. There was just enough light reflecting off the water to send ghostly shadows across our path. They teased our tired eyes and fooled our overwrought minds into thinking they were more than just tricks of light.

"What's that?" Dov cried, when a night bird rustled in the trees behind us.

"Is someone there?" Pellen whispered, when a cat leapt from a doorway into our path.

We made our way to the wharf in our own ghostly procession where my boat waited patiently, bobbing lazily against the dock.

"Go aboard," I told Pellen. "You can take Amyr into the cabin. There is a bunk for him to sleep. It will be much more comfortable than these hard benches.

"I'll help you," Dov insisted, anxiously jumping for the dock lines, when suddenly, behind us, we heard a man's voice.

"Halt!" he cried, illuminating the night with his torch. "Don't move or I'll shoot you! Stay where you are!"

"Who are you?" another voice demanded.

"Go quickly, Jan," Pellen hissed, as I climbed upon the foredeck and made to hoist my sail.

In the meantime, Dov had released all the lines and gave the boat a push with his foot. After which, he leapt into the air, landing squarely in the center of the boat. We rocked violently for a moment, as shots followed us from the shore.

"Go, Jan!" Pellen called again, grabbing the tiller and swinging it to and fro. Had I not been so busy trying to set the sail, I would have told him the rudder was not an oar and no amount of swaying would propel us any further.

"I can't," I cried instead, pulling the sail up as quickly as I could, but there was no wind to catch us, only the river's current to carry us out to sea.

"Stop!" the men yelled, their guns flashing brightly with yellow light. Something pinged against the mast, followed by a scream from Pellen.

"He's hit!" Dov called.

"Uncle?" I scrambled across the deck into the cockpit where Pellen was clutching his arm, blood running through his fingers like a sieve.

"Do something," Dov begged.

"I'm trying!" I pulled the tiller from Pellen's hand, and pushed him onto the cockpit floor where he lay stunned, watching the blood pool around him. His face had gone deathly white and his body began to shake.

"Take the boys to the motherland, Jan," he murmured. "No matter what happens to me."

Pointing the boat down river, I did my best to fill the sail, although it merely luffed and rippled, flapping like a useless wing. A shot pierced the sail and another hissed by my ear. "Get down!" I yelled to Dov and Amyr, who stood clutching the cabin door.

"Do something!" Dov demanded and for the second time, I thought he was speaking to me.

"I am! I am steering the boat. Get on the floor before you are hit, too. Take Amyr with you," I shouted, but neither boy paid any attention to my voice.

Dov was pulling Amyr forward, instead of down into the safety of the boat.

"What are you waiting for? Stop this now."

My cousin raised a hand, his palm outstretched as if to catch an unseen ball, and then, I saw a flash of bright white light.

From the shoreline, I heard an explosion, a thunderous boom followed by another, and accompanied by the rancid scent of burning flesh. At the same moment, my sails filled, a ferocious wind erupting from behind my back, catching us and propelling us forward at a rapid clip.

We raced down river as if we were flying. The sounds and scents from the explosion at the wharf receded into the past. With them, disappeared my mother and my auntie and all of my life in that tiny village.

Instead, I was embarking upon an adventure, a journey to a new life in the motherland across the sea with Pellen, Dov, and my cousin, Amyr, whose eyes shone like a million stars.

Just as we passed the mouth of the river, bursting out to the open sea, Amyr placed a hand upon my uncle's wound and healed it with his touch.

Chapter 9
Ailana

When I was eighteen years old, I was admitted to a university across the continent, surprising everyone, except for myself. It was in the outskirts of the Capitol City, a prestigious and well known institution, and I was very proud to have attained the rights to study there amongst the most learned professors and smartest students in the land.

"How will you pay?" Grandmother demanded, barely glancing up from the needlework in her lap. "I certainly can't afford it."

"I will find a way," I insisted. "I know I will."

"Better take your needle and thimble. You can always sew."

I would never sew. I would wait tables in a restaurant, or sweep the floors and polish the silver in the house of a great lady, long before I would submit again to hemming, darning, and tatting.

"Suit yourself," Grandmother said with a self-important sniff. "But, take this letter with a copy of my old royal commission. It will admit you into the service gates of the Imperial Palace where, at least, you'll be paid well for your toils. Now, thank me, you ungrateful child and give your old grandmother a kiss goodbye."

I did both, somewhat insolently and with little gratitude, although in hindsight, I have realized it was

Grandmother and her insistence that I take a needle, which brought the most cherished days of my life. Instead, at that moment, I left with anger in my heart for not once did she congratulate me on my acceptance. Not once did she say, 'Good work, Ailana.'

Neither did Embo, who was preoccupied with her little family and never cared much for me anyway. The feeling was mutual, although for Grandmother, we faked affection. Since the arrival of Embo's husband and baby, Taul, our precious space seemed overly cramped, as well as overly noisy.

Taul was a difficult infant, prone to screaming throughout the night, making it impossible for anyone to sleep. Neither could we work, or study during the day. We snapped at each other incessantly, blaming one another for our bad humor, which made an already difficult situation simply unbearable.

"One less person in this house is a good thing," Embo remarked, as the two of us air kissed and mumbled false words about how we might miss one another.

I took a bus across the continent, the cheapest means of travel I could afford, having saved coins from every bit of sewing in the last year. I rented a room in a boarding house adjacent to the university's campus, which included a shared bath, a well-worn cot, and access to a communal kitchen.

After settling in, I walked about the campus, relishing my new found freedom in this grand atmosphere of higher learning. My eyes soaked in the ancient stately buildings, the green swept lawns bordered by blossoming cherry trees and the beautiful, intelligent students congregating beneath them. I felt blessed to be here amongst them, although I considered myself just as worthy and smart. Unfortunately, neither my blessings, nor brains were sufficient to keep me there.

Within six months' time, I had run out of funds. Within six months' time, I was expelled from the university. In our tiny ghetto back in our little corner of Farku, my scholastic abilities were impressive. In this great university, in this once great Imperial city, my intelligence was only slightly above average, while my study habits were exceedingly poor.

It was my own fault. Never before had I been so far from my grandmother's protective wings with so much excitement at my disposal and the freedom to take advantage of it all. And, I did, for in my six months at the university, those learned professors taught me only one thing. I was part of the generation that would see our hopes dashed. We had lost both our parents and siblings to the Disease. We had watched the once brilliant Empire crumble around us, and with it, the promise of our future. The precipice was directly ahead, with a path guaranteed to be steep, so there was nothing to do but celebrate; drink, dance, and make love.

I took this lesson to heart and I partied with the best of them. I lived for the moment because they convinced me that was all I would have. The future was bleak, the learned men said. There was only now, and now would be gone by tomorrow, so live for today and never look back.

Six months later, I was alone, unable to pay for my room, with no classes to attend. My so-called friends had no use for me anymore either. Without my university admittance, I was no longer one of them. Instead, I became one of the many nobodies who lived upon the street.

It was spring then, and fortunately, a warm one, for without anywhere else, I found myself spending each night on a city park bench. That was if I could find an empty bench. Otherwise, a tree or patch of scraggly grass would do. Once or twice, I tried to sleep on cement.

During the day, I went in search of employment, something that was becoming more difficult to obtain, especially for a young Karut woman from Farku. At night, I lay wherever I might, my coat and small bindle bag as a blanket and pillow, staring at the sky and wondering where I would end up.

Sometimes, I would imagine myself in the motherland, a place I had never been to, nor ever desired to be. Yet, it gave me comfort in a way, imagining myself sleeping upon the forest floor, beneath these same stars, as my ancestors had done for centuries before. If they could survive as this, certainly, so could I. If they could brave the wild animals of the night, I could brave the creatures who roamed these city streets.

Although, I quickly became adept at defending both my person and place for the night, with Grandmother's needles and shears at the ready in my pocket, my homeless adventure ended quickly when the brief spate of warm spring weather turned into a deluge of torrential spring rain. The few shelters in the city quickly filled, as well as all doorways and abandoned buildings, thus increasing the urgency for me to find a place out of the storm.

I could return to Farku, but I was determined to avoid that at all costs. I would not go back and admit my failure, especially so soon. I resolved to keep trying, even if it meant I would take up the needle and thread again, and so with my grandmother's letter, I approached the Palace gates.

The guard took pity on me. That could be the only explanation for his generosity. I sincerely doubted that the recommendation of an elderly Karut woman, who had once sewn for the King's mother, held any weight. Neither was it my appearance, for I was wet and ragged, my hair knotted and filthy, my clothing dirty and torn. Still, I landed inside at the behest of the Royal Seamstress.

Living in the palace was little different from the university boarding house. In fact, the university was better, in that my bed was entirely mine. At the palace, I shared a bunk with two other girls, who I never saw awake, nor ever learned their names, although I knew one was a housemaid and the other, a cook.

The housemaid was tidy and after her, the sheets were always pulled tight and the bed nicely made. When her schedule briefly changed and the cook became the one who preceded me, she left a tiny mountain of crumbs, as fine as grains of sand, scattered throughout the sheets.

In our room, there were eleven other bunks with thirty-six girls overall to share the bathroom and showers. Our meals were taken in the servants' cafeteria and our two sets of uniforms were washed every week.

My job as seamstress-apprentice was to repair those same uniforms, for the staff had a habit of acquiring holes and tears. When I proved I could darn well enough or reweave with the best of them, I advanced to new construction where I sewed together caps.

Six months later, instead of acquiring a university education, I was promoted to the title of Seamstress and placed on the King's staff. Had there been a queen or even a princess, I might have preferred to design their beautiful gowns, but there was neither, both having been lost to the sickness several years prior.

Instead, I was given the King's own trousers to hem, his cuffs to take up or let down, his buttons to replace, his aiguillettes and epaulettes to reweave. For this, I was also given a purse full of coins, which on my weekly day-off, I took into the city and deposited in a bank.

I spent a few coins on clothes for myself, for on that day-off, I chose not to look like a seamstress-servant, but rather a woman of means enjoying herself about town. Once a week, I treated myself to a nice meal in a restaurant, and once every two months, I went to a salon and had my hair styled. It pleased me inordinately to pretend I was someone else here in the Capitol City amongst the planet's most well-to-do.

On one such day in the beginning of the autumn when the last of the sun's warmth was turning the marble building into a million shades of pink, I was returning from my outing to the city, strolling lazily among the palace grounds. I was reluctant to retire to my shared bed and the work day that would commence in precious few hours. The grounds looked so pretty and inviting, encouraging me to waste my sleep-time amongst them.

The icicle fountain, made entirely of glass, was turned on, an exceedingly rare occurrence in those days. Spewing brilliant streams of water, in every color imaginable, the structure rose from the courtyard like a giant mountain. Surrounding it were roses in as many colors as the fountain's streams. It was a magnificent sight to behold that night, made only more so by the rising of the two golden moons.

With a satisfied sigh, I sat down on a nearby bench, enjoying the music of the trickling waters and the emerging halo of the celestial lights overhead.

At that moment, I felt as if I was living in a world suddenly infused with magic. I did not regret any choice I had made then, despite having still a needle and a thread, instead of a university book in my hand.

"Do you mind if I sit down?" a man asked, interrupting my silent reverie and stealing my eyes away from the color-filled pageant before me.

I waved my hand dismissively, while at the same time sidling over to the edge of the bench, even though there was plenty of room for him and more.

He settled in, his weight shifting the bench slightly in his direction. For half a minute, he sat prone, as if holding his breath, his body filled with tension, before he moved again, leaning back, relaxing into his seat.

He coughed. He shifted his weight. He lifted one knee and crossed one leg over another. He fumbled in his pockets until he produced a cigarette.

"Do you mind?" he asked politely, his accent clipped and highly refined. "Or, may I offer you one?"

I shook my head. I didn't smoke, and neither did I care to have to breathe the exhalations of his.

"I would prefer that you did not contaminated the air which we much share," I replied haughtily, feigning the accent of the high-born, who lived in the beautiful suites above us, surrounding us on either side.

He paused, clearly startled by my reprimand, the cigarette flicking nervously between his fingers. The tension upon this bench increased, but I had claimed it first and would not willingly relinquish it without a fight.

Now, lighting the cigarette with a match he drew across the bench seat, he took a long drag before exhaling over his shoulder, the one opposite to me.

"I shall breathe this way," he remarked. "It shan't affect you. It shall not stain those beautiful teeth that you obviously prefer to hide."

I didn't deign to respond and instead of smiling, I profoundly frowned. I may have also sniffed a little, or made some other noise, for on his next drag, I heard him chuckle.

I tried to ignore him, preferring to watch the sunset and the ascent of the moons. I sat this way, my back turned to him until he finished his cigarette and tossed it on the ground. Smashing it with his foot, he leaned forward on the bench, running a hand through his waves of dark, disheveled hair, whereupon a wayward lock fell directly in front of his left eye.

"It is the last of the summer," he commented, trying to draw my attention back to him. "We are fortunate in this lovely night. I fear that soon the rains shall begin."

"Indeed," I muttered and though I tried not to look his way, I found myself studying him with the corner of an eye.

From where I sat, I could not discern the color of those eyes, or his curly hair, nor could I tell whether he was old or young, or if I knew his face.

"Did you know this fountain was originally commissioned by the Great Emperor for his beloved wife? This place was the very center of the courtyard of their once magnificent Imperial Palace."

I didn't know this and neither did I respond, which he took as a reason to continue his explanation.

"The roses that surround us were once a great garden, another testament to her. He was quite the romantic, the Great Emperor was, or at least, that is what we have been taught to believe."

"They had a great love," I said, rewarding him with these few chosen words.

"Indeed. Everyone should be so fortunate in this life."

I nodded, or maybe, I merely sat in silence, for there were no words which I could think to say. I had not been so fortunate and truly doubted that I ever would be. In fact, I doubted anyone was, or that the Emperor and Empress, nearly two centuries ago, were quite as magnificent or admirable as history had described.

"When I was a child," my companion continued, leaning back on the bench once again. "This fountain was always silent. The Empress Sara thought it wasteful to turn it on. A pity it was, for you can see how truly charming it is. For the cost of a few coins, I believe this beauty is well worth the price."

Now, the gentleman pulled himself to his feet in a manner of one who has toiled long and hard that day. Then, he dipped his head slightly in a bow, the sort a gentleman made to a lady of this court.

"Perhaps, we shall meet again. Tell me your name, young beautiful maid?"

"Ailana," I replied. "May I know yours, good sir?"

"Ailana." He dipped his head again. "It is a Karupta name, although your looks do not suggest it."

"I am of the motherland, although I have been raised in Farku, in the Duchy of Korelesk on the continent's western border."

"Ailana of Farku then," he replied, a tiny smile drawing upon his lips. "I shall enjoy seeing your beautiful smile in the daylight. I will look for you when the sun is out." Turning his back to me, the gentleman strode away.

"Your name, sir?" I reminded him. "It is only fair that I know with whom I speak."

"Of course," he called over his shoulder, telling me nothing more.

Chapter 10
Lance

Right after my disastrous attempt at romancing Nurse Moosy, I briefly, very briefly, fell for a spacewoman named Jill. She was an officer, a young lieutenant and although we had nothing in common other than our human genetics, somehow we ended up in bed.

It could have been that I was vulnerable and on the rebound after my failed Andorian love, or maybe, she pulled rank on me, ordering me into her bed. Alternatively, and most likely, I was drunk when we met in a bar. We were just two lonely galactic sailors looking for a night of companionship and love.

Actually, Jill and I spent more than a single night in a hotel room, but in hindsight, I couldn't recall exactly how many. We crossed paths several times at spacebases throughout the fourth sector and each time we met, we immediately went to bed.

Eventually, Jill transferred to the Columbia, which was stationed in the twelfth sector, thirty light years away. Our trysts ended then, and frankly, I forgot about her altogether, until out of nowhere she suddenly reappeared.

It was nine years later when we bumped into each other in the Officer's Club on Spacebase 37-D. During the intervening time, Wen, Noodnick, and I had all graduated from Officer Candidate School and were now commissioned and serving on the S/S Discovery.

Wen was a lieutenant, managing the storerooms on deck five, while Noodnick was still an ensign in engineering. As for me, somehow my previous affinity for laziness and slovenliness had been replaced with an aptitude to command. I had advanced to Lieutenant Commander and was serving on the bridge. Go figure.

At any rate, one afternoon while the ship was loading up stock, Noodnick and I had a few hours leave to waste in the spacebase bar, while Wen was occupied in his stores. Noodnick and I, although we had been friends for a number of years, had little to discuss, especially since he didn't speak. Still, his companionship was comfortable. Sitting with Noodnick was better than sitting alone. At least this is what I told myself whenever I tried, but failed to pick up a girl.

"Did I ever tell you why I joined SpaceForce?" I was saying, rolling my cold brewskie between my fingers, leaning my elbows on the bar and staring forlornly in the mirror.

I liked to drink my beers from the bottle since that bar on Spacebase 25-C where the barkeep was a wolf-man from the planet Canina IV. The guy was nice enough, and although he claimed it was efficient and ultra-hygienic, I just couldn't wrap my head around drinking from a glass cleaned by his long tongue.

Noodnick didn't respond. Frankly, if he had responded, I probably would have fallen off my stool. At any rate, I continued with my story assuming he was listening.

"I inherited this coin from my dad. It was an old Imperial dollar, and for a while there, it was the only thing of value that I owned. I wanted to cash it in, use whatever it was worth to pay my bills. I ended up keeping it, holding on to it for old time's sake. I don't know if it's worth anything or not. What do you think, Nood? Do you know anything about those kind of things?"

Noodnick sipped his drink. He drank beer through a straw, which for some odd reason, the chicks seemed to find very attractive. I supposed, Noodnick wasn't a bad looking guy, despite his lack of conversation, but why the girls swarmed around him, I never understood. They'd grab the empty stools by his side, talk endlessly as if he was listening, rub his arm and proposition him, while completely ignoring me. He must have been emitting pheromones or doing something I couldn't see. Whatever it was, the dude was one lucky bastard, while I was a loser no matter how hard I tried.

"I was hoping in our travels, we might be going by the old Empire, and then I could ask someone about it, but after more than a decade in space, I've never been called into that sector."

Of course, Noodnick didn't respond to this either, or to the woman who was insisting she would buy him another drink. I wondered if I just shut up, kept my mouth completely closed, never saying a word, would I get as lucky as this schmuck?

Probably not, I decided, glancing in the bar's mirror, spying Wen as he wandered in through the door.

"Oh hey, Lancelot!" Wen called, waving wildly as if I hadn't seen him two hours ago.

I removed my cap from the neighboring stool, but before Wen could get halfway across the room, another person plopped herself down by my side.

"Jill!" I gasped, recognizing her instantly.

Actually, that was a lie. I only recognized her by the name tag snapped to her chest. She wore captain's bars and a patch from the S/S Asteroid, which was about the stupidest name assigned to any ship.

At any rate, I made room for her and expressed my pleasure at this odd coincidence. Actually, that was a lie too, as I wasn't at all that happy to see her again. In fact, if it weren't for Wen taking Noodnick's newly vacated seat and refreshing my brew, I would have gotten up and left in a hurry.

"Lt. Commander," Jill said coldly, which had nothing to do with the icy shot of vodka in her hand.

Regarding me in the mirror with narrow, judgmental eyes, I saw a trace of disgust flit across her face. I might have been looking at her in the same way. With added lines to her face and gray scattered throughout her hair, I was thinking she hadn't aged all that well either. With the two of us scowling at our reflections, it was a fair bet that we weren't going to end up in bed this time.

"What a coincidence," I exclaimed, raising my new bottle in a mock toast.

"Not at all," Jill replied, knocking back her shot. "Come with me."

"Yes, Ma'am!" Maybe, I was wrong? Come to think of it, Jill didn't look half bad. In a hurry, I gulped my beer, figuring with the lights off, we could pretend the intervening years had never happened. I followed her out of the bar, winking at Wen, who watched us with surprise. I waved to Noodnick who was now closeted in a booth with three young women. Noodnick didn't say anything, of course, and I may have been wrong, but I think I saw him give me a *thumbs up.* "So, where to, Captain?" I asked, sauntering a little.

"Shut up," she growled and led me down the mall to a pizza parlor called, *Chunk o' Cheese.*

Once, on another spacebase, the guys and I had gone in there to look for girls. Wen had read an article that said family restaurants were a good pickup place. It might have been, but we didn't stay long enough to find out. Frankly, the place looked toxic. We couldn't hear ourselves talk, let alone think. The pizza tasted like someone had baked it in grease scraped off the floor and every few minutes, some animatronic animals started singing and dancing in the middle of the room.

"Uh, Jill," I called, over the ruckus. "If you want pizza, there's a better place two decks down."

"Shut up!" she snapped again, which I clearly heard despite the dancing drumbeat of a pair of animatronic mice.

Jill hurried to the furthest corner of the room, to a small booth. There sat a young girl, smiling at the dancing idiots, and nibbling on a pizza.

"Hi," the girl called to me, turning the most amazing pair of emerald green eyes upon my face. "Are you my dad?"

"Uh…no. Not me."

"Oh." She frowned, "That's too bad. I like you. You seem nice."

Gazing down at the sea of bright red hair spilling across her shoulders in wild curls, I decided I liked her, too, surprising myself with this thought. Never before had I cared for any kid. In my mind, children were a necessary nuisance ranking slightly below Wen and Noodnick, and significantly below dogs when it came to my choice of companion. Furthermore, there was no way I could be her dad. Nobody that beautiful could ever be related to me.

Glancing back at Jill, who was looking at her cell, I concluded that nobody that beautiful could be related to her either.

"I've got to go," Jill mumbled, pecking the kid on the top of her curly head. Then, she glared at me. "Good luck, Lance." She snickered, and rushed away before I could protest.

So, there I was, alone with the little chick and her 15" pie.

"She'll be right back in a minute, I'm sure." I nodded and forced a smile, while glancing at the uneaten pepperoni and cheese. Was I hungry enough to risk my good health? Already there was a thick pool of grease forming on top.

The girl blinked her emerald eyes and nodded as if she knew. Setting her pizza back on her plate, she turned her attention to the hideous fake mice.

"There you are!" Wen cried, at exactly the same moment the mice finished their song. "I thought I saw you go in here. You hate this place, right, Lance? Remember that time we found a rat tail in the supreme combo on Spacebase 25-C?"

"Wen."

"Three years ago, I think. It was right after that cruise through the thirty-seventh sector."

"No! I'm saying your name, not asking you when it was. I remember when it was even though I've tried to block it out."

"Why?"
"Wen!"
"What?"

The child started to laugh. Her freckled cheeks turned a rosy, pink hue as the music bubbled from her throat.

"You guys are funny!" she cried, clapping her hands with delight. "I like you both. Are you sure you're not my dad?"

"No," I snapped.

"Are you going to finish this?" Wen asked, sitting down in the booth and gladly helping himself to a slice.

Then, the music and dancing started again, this time with chickens who were even uglier than the mice. Wen smiled broadly, clapping his hands in rhythm with the girl. I, on the other hand, was starting to get a headache, a bad one, which would require at least two migraine pills, or a significant amount of alcohol.

I collapsed in the seat across from Wen and Little Red, wondering how much longer until Jill returned. Furtively, I glanced at my watch every few seconds.

"This is great!" Wen proclaimed.

Little Red giggled. At least she was having fun.

"Yep," I replied.

Jill didn't return. An hour later, the pizza gone, Little Red leaning sleepily against Wen's shoulder, I glanced across the restaurant, catching a glimpse of a starship outside. The Asteroid was written across her side.

"What the fuck?" I shouted to the consternation of the parents at the neighboring table. Bolting from the booth and racing to the window, I watched the

Asteroid drift away from my view. "Wen, does that say Asteroid?"

"Sure does," Wen exclaimed.

"Goodbye, Mommy," the girl called, waving her hand.

"She left you here?" I gasped.

The child shrugged and blinked her eyes, great limpid pools as green as the oceans on Talas III. Like the oceans, they were wet, filling with tears, threatening to dribble down her cheeks.

"I'll call my commanding officer and get the ship to come back. Don't worry, kid, we'll make your mommy come get you."

"She won't. She told me goodbye." The girl sniffed and reached up with her thin arms. "Pick me up, Daddy. I'm tired and I want to go home."

"Wen?" I called.

"Now." Little Red yawned. "Please Daddy. Let's go to your ship."

"No, I mean, Wen!" I shouted at my friend, who had gone back to watch the animatronics do their thing. I wasn't sure what type of animal was dancing now, other than they appeared insanely weird. They each had three heads, seven legs, two tails and reproductive organs. Frankly, they shouldn't have been dancing with children present to watch their anatomically correct organs swing. Instinctively, I put my hand over Little Red's eyes. "Wen! Get over here!"

"What?" Reluctantly, he turned back to me, a crazy smile on his lips and a deep purple blush creeping up his cheeks.

"This kid---uh---" I realized I didn't even know her name.

"Sandy," she murmured, her arms still outstretched. "Pick me up. I'm tired."

"Come on, Wen," I announced, reaching for the kid and hefting her across my shoulder, where she promptly wrapped her arms around my neck and laid down her head. Striding past the animatronics, I headed out into the busy mall. "Jill abandoned Sandy. What kind of a mother does that? We've got to take her to the base's police station. I'm sure they've got some kind of social services there."

"That's terrible," Wen agreed, his eyes still glancing back at the dancing naked things.

"What a b-i-t-c-h," I continued, spelling for Sandy's benefit. "I mean, what sort of cruel parent would do that to this beautiful child?"

"But, I wasn't abandoned," Sandy murmured sleepily. "Mommy said it was time for my daddy to take care of me." Then, she shoved her nose into my neck and started to snore.

"We'll have to find him," I declared, although I kept my voice at a whisper. Poor baby needed her rest instead of traipsing around this spacebase looking for some dude.

"Uh---Lancelot," Wen started to say, stopping in the middle of the shopping hordes, nearly becoming trampled by a family of Cascadians, each nine-foot tall.

"What?"

He waggled his finger back and forth, his mouth once again smiling in a goofy way. I turned to see what he was waving at, expecting the anatomically correct animatronics to have followed us into the mall.

"What? What are you pointing at?"

"You, Lance. You're her father."

"No way!" I shouted, nearly dropping the kid on the concrete floor.

After that, I picked up my pace, running to the spacebase's administrative offices. I figured they could direct me to the police or whoever would care.

Naturally, it was after hours and the offices were closed, except for emergencies, in which case I had to pick up the red phone and dial zero.

"Lance?" Wen asked, just as I was reaching for that phone. "What are you doing?"

"I'm calling the authorities."

Naturally, the phone was dead. No dial tone. No numbers to push. No operator to ask me what in the hell I wanted.

"Fuck," I exhaled, leaning against the wall and shifting the sleeping child to my other shoulder, as the one she was drooling on had started to ache.

"She's very pretty. She looks just like you, except for---well---she's a girl and she has red hair and green eyes and looks completely different. I mean---"

"Shut up, Wen," I sighed. "We'll take her back to the ship and let SpaceForce Command figure this out."

I had thought that Command would compel Jill to take Sandy back. Abandoning her child was an action unbecoming of an officer. Of course, the same could be said for me, because sure enough, DNA tests proved that Sandy was mine. So, there I was, a brand new father to an eight year old girl.

I was given a new cabin with a tiny closet of a bedroom for my daughter and she was enrolled in the ship's school and daycare programs. At night, we would eat together with Wen and Noodnick in the family dining center, along with all of the other crew who had kids aboard.

It was a little difficult at first getting used to this little person in my life. Sandy loved to watch the vid and monopolized it whenever she was in our cabin. She also liked to lock herself in the bathroom and lay in a bubble-filled tub for hours on end, leaving me to run down three decks to use Wen's toilet whenever I had to go.

Having Sandy around did bring a few benefits, though, some that I could never have imagined. To all the single women aboard, I suddenly looked like an awesome father. They flocked around me and the kid, asking me out on dates even though they had refused me before. Nearly every weekend, Noodnick or Wen was called upon to babysit.

A couple years later, after I had been promoted to full commander, when Sandy was in the fifth grade, or thereabouts, the Discovery was reassigned to patrol the fourth sector. We were near the boundaries of what had been the old Empire, orbiting a moon which had an amusement park that Sandy was sure to like.

We were heading out on shore-leave with Wen and Noodnick, when I discovered that old coin sitting in my dresser drawer. On a whim, I put it in my pocket.

"Hey, I wonder if anyone on this moon will be able to tell me how much it's worth." I was talking mostly to myself, but Sandy overheard.

"What?" She turned her gaze away from that show on the vid, which featured a bunch of kids singing in some high school auditorium. Once again, I marveled at how incredibly beautiful my child was. No matter how many times I looked at her, my Sandy had the appearance of a red-headed angel.

"I've got this coin." Fishing it out of my pocket, I began to explain about my inheritance and how I had intended to take it to the old Empire. "So, I've been in space for nearly a dozen years, and this is the first time I've gotten anywhere close. Maybe someone will make me an offer for ten thousand dollars or more."

"May I see it, Daddy?"

"Sure."

I laid it in her hand. It was gold and heavy. Despite its age and wear, the etchings were still quite clear. The backside had the Imperial Crest with the black eagle and two crossed swords. Displayed on the front, in profile, was the old emperor's face.

Sandy looked at it in her palm and her mouth fell open wide. Her big green eyes instantly filled with tears.

"What is it?" I cried as her hand began to shake.

"I lost this," she wailed. "This was mine."

Chapter 11
Pellen

We had traveled across the sea for nearly seven days when the peaks of the Blue Mountains came into sight. This was quicker than I had imagined, for the distance to our motherland had always seemed as far as the next star, and as difficult a journey as traversing through space. The winds had blown strongly and from behind us, swelling Jan's torn sail as if their sole purpose was to propel us to the awaiting shore. This made our passage easy. The boat rocked little and though it was small, there seemed to be room enough for us four.

The rains came each day, but only briefly, filling our bucket with just enough to wash and quench our thirst. Jan and the little orphan, Dov fished often, their nets trailing behind us in the morning when the currents were calm and the fish climbed to the surface in search of food.

For our meals, we shared their catch, carving it into small pieces, devouring the raw salty flesh as if it was the finest of delicacies served in the land.

My son enjoyed this menu, much more so than the thin soups and flat, stale breads he was accustomed to at home. Whether as a result of the proteins in this flesh or the irons in the fish blood he sipped, Amyr remained strong during those few days, sitting upright, or walking slowly about the boat. In my haste to depart, I had forgotten all his medicines at home, yet now, without them, he seemed healthier than before. His strange, but beautiful eyes, glowed like a brilliant rainbow of light, although there was a new darkness in them, a coldness, as if his joy was gone.

"What is it?" I would ask him. "What troubles you, my son?"

"Nothing, Papa," he would murmur, turning away.

My son was changing on this voyage, metamorphosing in a way I could not understand. It was ever so slightly, almost unnoticeable until I blinked and then, I could not say exactly what was different.

This I knew, always, despite his lifetime of frailness and infirmity, Amyr had a peace about him, a smile upon his face. He was loving and we cherished him. Inexplicably, his very presence seemed to fill us with hope. Now, I felt a chill whenever I gazed upon his face. My lips froze when I kissed his forehead. My hand stopped and refused to touch, when I reached to stroke his beautiful hair.

"Leave me be, Papa."

He dismissed me, turning his back when only days before I had clutched him to my chest. I feared I was losing him, when in truth, to me he was already gone. Only days before, I had a wife and son and now I was alone with neither a family, nor a home, journeying across the massive sea to a land unknown.

What became of my wife, I could only guess. For weeks prior, in the village, I had heard rumors that made my heart sicken. If Ailana was alive when the Korelesk's army found her, I shuddered to imagine what they did. My wife, despite her thin form, and the new cruelness in her heart, was still beautiful, so much so, all others paled beside her.

I had also heard tales of camps and prison like places where our people were taken and put to work. I didn't know much of these things as only snippets were passed in the whisperings between one and another.

Of course, all of it could be false, I had told myself. In this time and this century, I could not imagine my fellow man so uncivilized and cruel. This was before the army came to our doors. This was before our village was reduced to rubble and ash, and I was set adrift upon the ocean.

I was thankful beyond measure that we had come safely to this boat and that our travels on this sea were going well. Each night, I bid these children to join me in prayer, to thank the Holy One for His guidance and His grace. Although we didn't know the words, having never spoken the language of the motherland, I believe we communicated these thoughts in our hearts.

Dov and Jan joined me in this worship, kneeling by my side, bowing their heads and holding hands, closing their eyes. Amyr sat on the forward deck, purposely avoiding us and our prayer, his odd eyes flashing in the darkness at the sea.

"Is he not grateful?" Jan asked after bidding him to take her hand, to which he shook his head and resumed his perch on the bow.

"Of course, he is," I began to say.

"He prays in his own way," the street boy replied with a knowing certainty in his voice and in his eyes.

"How?"

The little boy shrugged. "Leave him alone. You won't understand even if he tells you."

"And, how do you know?" Jan demanded. "The two of you have only just met."

Dov smiled. "Like him, I am an old soul, as old as the wind, as old as the sea. Amyr and I have crossed paths many times in other lives."

Our travels were filled with endless hours of boredom when I grew restless, for there was little for me to do. I would have fished or guided the boat, but my skills were poor, while the children took pleasure in these tasks.

Instead, I stared at the horizon and reflected upon my arm. I had been shot, yet I showed no trace of wound. I had seen both blood and bone and felt the searing pain. A moment later, I saw and felt nothing amiss.

Had I imagined it all, the healing touch from my son's hand? Jan and Dov had seen it too for days afterward, Jan insisted upon examining my arm.

I did not dare approach my son and question him, despite how it consumed my thoughts both day and night. However, my wife's parting words resonated through my skull. He was not my son. He never was. But, who did he belong to then, and why was he here?

Now, I could see not only was this true, but entirely obvious, had I dared to look. He resembled nothing of me, not in his beauty or his temperament. I had always attributed his looks to Ailana's fair genes, assuming her father had granted him the wavy black hair, the noble brow, the firm chin, and the strangely colored eyes.

"Jan," I whispered to my niece one night, while we lay awake staring at the vast star-filled sky and bathing in the light of the two moons. "Have you ever seen a picture of Ailana's father, or your grandfather, perhaps?"

"No, Uncle. Why do you ask?"

At first, I didn't respond, for to do so would be to admit out loud that which I truly didn't want to know.

Jan hesitated, and her breath came quickly, which I knew meant she had something to say.

"Tell me," I bid her with a sigh. "It doesn't matter anyway. I will always love him as my son. I will always love you, my niece, the same as if you were my daughter."

Jan drew a long deep breath and exhaled slowly, speaking to the stars, refusing to meet my gaze.

"I shouldn't," she insisted. "What Mama told me was a secret not to be shared."

I nodded, although she did not see it. Revealing this was nearly the same as exposing the secret itself.

"Mama said Amyr takes after his father. Mama said had she not been present and seen Auntie give birth, she would have doubted that Auntie was even his mother. I am sorry, Uncle. You have been the best father to him, and to me, for I can recall so little of my own papa."

I patted Jan's hand and rose unsteadily. The boat rocked beneath me as it bobbed up and down on the waves. The winds were calm, but the current was strong, and we still moved along with a steady clip as I stood grasping the rail and watching Amyr.

He was laying upon the boat's bow. Dov sat next to him, their feet side by side. Their hands were behind their heads, their faces upturned to the darkened sky.

I saw then in the light of the two moons, everything that I missed in the daylight of the sun. My son, my heart, my babe was the issue of another man, and with a face that was recognizable by another name.

The next morning a large boat approached us from the shore. Aboard were our kinsmen, although they did not know it. They pointed their guns upon us and shouted in a language I didn't understand.

The children waved and called, but the men didn't lower their guns until Amyr climbed from the tiny cabin where he had been asleep. I didn't know if it was his face that caused such shock, his fluency in a language he had never once uttered, or the brightly colored light shining from his eyes.

"Kari-fa!" a man declared, his voice carrying across the waves.

He stepped back from the rail and spoke quickly to his comrades. The only word I understood was the exclamation at the outset of his sentence. It was a profanity my grandfather often used and one I would not repeat in the presence of these children.

However, he was not the only one to utter this expletive. His companions pointed at my son and cried the same, reminding me again how blind and foolish I had been. What was clearly obvious to these strangers had eluded me for more than ten years.

In the end, the Karuptas laid down their guns and welcomed us aboard their vessel. Towing Jan's little craft along behind, I wondered how the four of us crossed the ocean in such a tiny boat without being swamped by waves or capsized by a gust of wind.

Several hours later when we stood unsteadily upon the shore, our feet unused to the earth after so long at sea, I marveled again how we came to escape, while our friends and neighbors were now dead or enslaved.

I knelt upon the dirt of this holy land from which my forefathers and mothers sought so anxiously to leave and I, just as anxiously or more so, had longed to return.

"Kira-ka tefira laka lanu," a man said as I let the soil sift through my fingers.

I shrugged and shook my head, apologizing for my lack of comprehension. He repeated his words louder as if it was only his volume that kept me from comprehending.

"He says you have been blessed," Amyr announced from his side.

"By who?" I asked, as my son walked away.

He left with the men of Karupatani, leaving me alone with neither wife, nor child.

"He belongs with them," Dov said taking my hand in his. "You have done your part and now it is time for someone else."

"You have us, Uncle," Jan said. "And, we are home. We are your family."

Thus, it was, and I told myself, I would be content. I was, for here amongst my people, I was meant to be.

Chapter 12
Ailana

In the winter, I was given the King's cloak to mend after his horse had stepped upon the hem and torn it out. While I was repairing this unfortunate occurrence, I was asked to change the buttons from gold to black.

"He means to melt and sell the gold," the Head Seamstress reported. "Our treasury is so empty. Even as a lad, poor Mikal was never good with counting sums." This was followed by a series of clucks that the old woman made with her tongue. "Back in the Empress Sara's day, Mikal's father, Duke Thunk had quite the grasp on our finances. Not only could they wear their fancy gold buttons, but every Sunday was a special dinner just for palace staff. I remember the desserts. Always, there were enormous, fancy cakes, and fountains that poured chocolate like water."

I liked the black buttons, even more so than the gold, but I did not argue with the Head Seamstress, who was always right. The buttons were made from onyx, soft and shiny and as smooth as pearls. They were cool to my touch, as soothing as water upon my fingers.

I lingered over this task, sewing each button with extraordinary care for it was the King who would touch these after me. Then, I hemmed his cape with a precision that even my grandmother would envy, letting the heavy waves of soft cashmere keep me warm.

The winter was wicked, as bad as any had ever been with great storms blowing upon us from the ocean. It snowed heavily for weeks, and when that stopped, it rained just as hard. The river flooded the city streets as the sea did the same to the courtyard of the palace.

With the floods, those so unfortunate to be living upon the streets, were swept off in the waters like specks of dirt. My old companions in the parks were washed away, never more to be seen.

"And not missed, I tell you," the Head Seamstress cackled. "Better they be gone."

In the spring, the waters receded and for a while, the city looked clean, although there was an undercurrent of fear even within the safety of the palace gates.

"Duke Korelesk is angry," the Head Seamstress declared, biting off a thread she had used to repair a fine lady's dress. The lady was the wife of the late Duke of Turko, and some said she was at the palace to romance the King. "The King let so many die, even though I say good riddance. Korelesk would have done nothing different, but he uses it to gain political points."

"Why?" I asked, threading my own needle to repair a workman's trousers. The King's fine clothes needed nothing these days. Either he never wore them, or the dowager Duchess Turko was repairing them herself.

"Korelesk sees himself as king. If our Mikal does not wake from his malaise and raise a hand against his enemies, we'll be sewing for Korelesk and his bastard offspring."

Korelesk himself was a bastard, his claim to the throne dating back to an illegitimate prince from centuries prior. None of that would matter though. If Mikal died and Korelesk seized the throne, there would be no one to challenge Korelesk's new rule of law.

"Except for the new Duke of Turko, that odd alien fellow, whatever he is, and the Duke of Kildoo, who is an ancient, elderly man. Oh, what a state we are in!" The Head Seamstress declared, "It was so much better during the Empress Sara's days, and before that, during the time of the Great Emperor, her grandfather."

I would have liked to tell my mistress how much she sounded like my grandmother and how it irritated me in the same way. But, I didn't. It was spring and the flowers were in bloom. Each morning I awoke in my shared bed to the music of birds chirping.

I didn't care about Korelesk or even our King Mikal. I cared only for myself and the attention of young men who would follow me about the courtyard, or approach me in the restaurants where I dined.

The fountain had been turned off since the autumn, since that night when I was joined upon a bench by a gentleman, who smoked a cigarette. Not once since then had I seen him, but neither did I care.

Still, I loved to stroll the city streets, and the palace grounds, especially when the daylight lasted well into the evening. Gentlemen and their lessers would sidle to my side and bow politely, inquiring if I might be joined. Whether or not I consented, they'd remark upon the weather, or my lovely dress, or the brilliant golden color of my hair. Always, they asked my name and only rarely would I answer. Yet, they followed me as if I had a train.

During a night of the golden moons, when the sky shone with a color that some said was the same as my hair, there was a chill to the air despite being well into the spring. I was standing and admiring the scent of a new white rose, leaning into the bush, my nose perfectly positioned to inhale the blossom's delicate fragrance, when someone bumped squarely into me, knocking me ajar. I fell upon the rosebush, becoming entangled in its thorns, whereupon I tore my wrap and scratched both hands and face.

"I beg your pardon!" a man cried. "I am so sorry for what I have done. I confess, I was not paying attention to where I was walking." He reached for my arm, which I immediately pushed away.

However, in attempting to brush him off, I caught my sleeve upon his cuff and in the ensuing awkward effort to untangle ourselves, I tore off his button. Once free, he bowed politely, and then, hurried away upon the path, while I swore profusely in the language of the motherland. That was until I looked upon the button in my hand, or rather ran my fingers across its smooth and shiny surface.

"Kari-fa!" I said aloud, for the King's black onyx button shimmered like the golden moonlight overhead.

I kept the button, although I told no one, storing it in my purse among with my coins. It wasn't worth much, but when I gazed upon it I always laughed, for it reminded me of how I fell into a rosebush at the behest of the King.

During the summer months, I began to see a young man. We met on the palace steps one balmy evening, both returning from the old city at the same time. Lioter had been raised in the palace, as his father was a confidant to the king. In fact, all of his grandfathers, dating back to the one who served the Great Emperor, made a living of whispering into the King's ear.

"In whose ear shall you whisper?" I asked, on our third date, when Lioter took me to a pub near my old university campus.

Initially, I had been hesitant to return, afraid to see again my learned former companions. I dressed overly well for that evening, wearing my most expensive outfit from a high-fashion shop and clinging tightly to Lioter's arm for he looked quite grand.

Speaking with the refined, noble accent of one who lived in a palace apartment which faced the sea, Lioter smiled at me and raised his glass of beer.

"I shall whisper into the ear of the next king," he declared. "To Marko Korelesk, who shall succeed our own hapless, but beloved, Mikal, when he passes from this world to the next."

"How can you be so certain that either event shall come to pass?" the gentleman resting upon the barstool next to Lioter interrupted our conversation. "Mikal may be hapless, but at last check, he seemed quite healthy."

"I beg to differ, sir," my date replied, swiveling around so that his back was to me. "Have you seen

Mikal lately? His looks are dreadful. He hangs his head like a lost dog, his shoulders bent already in defeat. I have heard his voice never raises above a mumble, and when he speaks, his words are barely comprehensible. My lord, Duke Marko Korelesk, on the other hand, brims with energy and good health."

"Is that so?" the gentleman replied, sipping his own glass and staring reflectively in the mirror. I glanced around Lioter, but could see nothing of his neighbor's features, for the gentleman was wearing a dark cloak and large hat. However, his voice was vaguely familiar, and at first, I believed him to be a professor that I had known. "How come you to know so well of either man, young friend?"

Lioter smiled and leaned back upon his stool, already having swallowed more beer than he should. He proceeded to wax eloquently of the esteemed positions of his forbears, as well as his own efforts to insinuate himself in the service of Duke Marko.

"I am already a good friend of the Duke's Chief of Staff," Lioter bragged, "Even though I am an under-under secretary to the King."

"So, you are a spy of sorts," the gentleman concluded, while I decided that Lioter's revelation to this stranger was a bit imprudent.

"I suppose so," Lioter chuckled, and waved for another glass. "You seem intelligent, sir, and your accents speaks of noble lineage. If you would like, I could introduce you to the Duke's service. I require only a tiny recompense for this favor, which undoubtedly as a man of obvious high blood, you shall reap a great benefit from this acquaintance. Perhaps, when King Marko sits the throne, you shall be a Lord Advisor."

The stranger laughed wholeheartedly, setting down his cup. Rising to his feet, he tossed three coins upon the counter.

"You assume that I am not of the nobility already?"

"If you were, why would you be wasting your time and precious coins on this dreadful beer?" Lioter shook his glass. "You would be drinking the finest brews at the Imperial Palace, where the pubs are much nicer than this."

"Indeed," the stranger replied. "But, this pub is far more entertaining. Look how I have had the good fortune to become acquainted with you and the lovely lady sitting by your side. For the pleasure of your company, allow me to pay for your beer." Then, he tipped his head to me and began to walk away.

"Ha!" Lioter declared. "We are in luck."

"No, we aren't," I replied, for my blood had suddenly gone cold.

As the stranger departed the busy pub, I realized who he was. I recognized the cloak, for it was my own handiwork upon the hem, and the shiny onyx buttons, which graced his cuffs, matched the lost one in my pocket.

Lioter was executed three days later, after a rapid trial for treason and a sentencing at the behest of the King. I was spared, although I knew not why. I returned to work and I slept in my shared bed, but I did not walk the gardens or wander the city alone. I was afraid. Someone was following me.

Each time I turned my neck, I spied a shadow in the corner of my eye. After a week unable to sleep and jumping at every sound, I was summoned into the King's office by a guardsman.

"Oh my! What is that about, I wonder?" the Head Seamstress muttered, as I rose from my sewing table to follow the guard.

He escorted me into the Big House, the building in which the King resided, and guided me up a marble staircase to a heavy, ornate door. From there, I was admitted into an office, followed by another where I sat in a plush leather chair and waited for an hour.

By the time I was granted entrance into the King's inner sanctum, I was ready to faint from both fear and exhaustion, but I didn't. I held my back straight and my head high as I walked in. After all, my grandmother had been a Royal Seamstress to his mother.

King Mikal sat behind an immense and elegant wooden desk upon which were piled stacks of papers. Behind him were windows gazing out at the sea. To my left was a fireplace with an immense stone hearth. Directly in front of the fire, a man was reclining on a sofa. He smiled while raising a glass of amber wine as if in toast to me. Dutifully, I curtseyed firstly to the King and then, the gentleman.

"Ailana," the King said. "Ailana of Farku in the Duchy of Korelesk, from the tiny Karupta ghetto, upriver from the sea."

I raised my eyes to his face and recognized the gentleman from the fountain bench, nearly a year past.

"Pleased to meet you, Ailana of Farku," the nobleman from the sofa declared, tipping back his head and swallowing the liquid from his cup. "Come closer so I may see you. From this distance, you are quite pretty, but your name bespeaks a Karut, which personally, I don't favor."

I looked again to the King, who nodded and bid me cross the floor.

"You don't realize what you miss, Marko," the King replied, rising to pour his own glass. "And, I believe your blood of the motherland is even less diluted than mine."

Marko, Duke Korelesk, laughed heartily and smiled, bringing his cup again to his lips. I found him repulsive, his overbearing stomach which nestled like a large ball upon his hips, and his jowls which swung from side to side as he moved his mouth. His hair was long and thin, and although, I assumed his hygiene was well kept, his tresses appeared unwashed, and direly in need of a cut and style. Only the Duke's eyes were interesting, for they were so light as to almost be devoid of color, but now they judged me harshly with no pleasure.

"Don't remind me," the Duke scoffed, as the King refilled his cup. "She is pretty, Mike. A beautiful smile, above all else. Show me your teeth, girl. I always look upon my filly's teeth before I mount."

Dutifully, I forced my lips upward, although my feet, like a filly's were inclined to kick.

"Very pretty" the Duke repeated, "but, rather skinny. Surely, you have a mare or even a colt in your stable who can offer me a better ride."

"This one is unbroken. I thought you preferred them that way."

"Ah! Well, perhaps now, I might reconsider."

"Nay. You, a new father of a strapping son, must be dutiful to your wife for a least a week."

"Ach. If I am lucky, she will perish quickly of the Disease. As to my son, had he not arrived with a cock, I would have thought him born a girl. You do not realize how fortunate you have been, Mike. I should gladly change places, just say the word. Ah, how I wish I was like you, unattached and unfettered."

The King chuckled. "How you wish you might change places and wear my crown."

Now, the Duke laughed and his eyes once again surveyed my body.

"Perhaps, I will take her. The more I gaze upon her, the more I like."

Too late." The King waved his hand, much to my relief. "Leave us now, Marko. You may find the barn beyond the fence to the south of the main gate. There we have a donkey and an ass or two that you might enjoy. You may stay, Mistress Ailana of Farku. I should like to speak with you alone."

The Duke chuckled and leered as if the King's intentions were not honorable.

"Let me know how it goes, cousin," the duke called, rising to his feet and strolling to the door. "If you change your mind, I suppose I can close my eyes. All cats are black at night, even Karut ones."

I was not sorry to see the Duke depart, although I grew nervous alone in the King's presence. I shouldn't have. Why, we had met already thrice before, and each time, the King had treated me with respect. However, he had swiftly and bloodthirstily executed my friend, Lioter, so despite his calm demeanor and appearance, I would not let down my guard.

"Would you care for a drink, Ailana of Farku?" he asked, offering me a glass, a tiny smile playing upon his lips. "Please. It is the least I may do for having forced you to come to this dark and dreary office. Can you feel the ghosts surrounding us? There are so many, it is nearly impossible to breathe. One must fortify themselves, lest we let them infect our souls."

"The ghosts?" I accepted the cup and sipped slowly of the amber liquid. It went straight to my head and made me cough, but also filled my tongue with boldness, much more so than it should have.

"This was my great-grandfather's office, the Great Emperor. Of course, you know of whom I speak. If you were summoned here it was either because he liked you, or because he meant to dispatch your soul himself. Let me tell you, there were very few he liked. Beneath this fine carpet, many red stains cross these floors. Now, why don't you tell me what you know of Korelesk's plans."

"And, if I refuse, do you mean to dispatch me? I find little difference in your treatment of my friend, Lioter, and the conduct of your esteemed, but violent ancestor. Perhaps, you resemble him in more ways than just your looks."

For a moment, the King seemed taken aback. His dark eyes narrowed and at first, his mouth turned down.

"You are a brazen little one, aren't you?" he murmured, breaking into a smile. "It is a trait of those who hail from the motherland. But, I have asked you a question. Now, I bid you take advantage of the hospitality I have extended. Seat yourself upon my sofa, and tell me what you know."

He strolled over to the hearth and stood with his back to me, contemplating the flames and the shadows they cast upon the walls. I took a place upon the sofa across from where the Duke had been, watching the King from beneath my lashes, as he waited for information I did not have.

Mikal was always a handsome man, in the manner of his forbearers, but his eyes were dark and filled with disappointment. Despite the differences in our station and age, and despite his poor treatment of my friend, I found myself gazing upon him with pity, for clearly he was unhappy in this life.

"I know nothing," I told him, as convincingly as I could. "I have not met the Duke of Korelesk before this day."

"But, your friend, the spy knew him quite well. Are you certain you had not made the Duke's acquaintance in his company?"

"No! I knew nothing of Lioter's friends or political leanings, as our conversations were always quite innocent and of no particular topic."

"What did you discuss in these conversations?"

"I don't recall," I replied honestly. "Not much of anything. Perhaps, we discussed flowers as we walked about the gardens in the evenings."

"Flowers?"

"He appreciated the vast collection in the rose garden."

"Roses," the King repeated and upon his lips there grew a smirk. "I believe you, Miss Farku, for you are far too innocent to engage in games of high intrigue. You may finish your wine and depart from my company."

"Thank you, Sir," I said, swallowing the dregs at the bottom of my glass. "Might I ask what you were doing in the pub that night? Surely, there are finer establishments where a man of your station might enjoy a drink?"

"You are also presumptuous, Miss Farku," the King laughed. He leaned against the hearth and reached into his pocket, extracting a cigarette. "Upon our first meeting, you criticized my desire to smoke, while on our second, you showed disdain for my choice of pubs."

"I mean no offense, Sir," I cried. "I was merely curious as to why you would venture to that part of town. And, this is our fourth meeting, for you did collide with me in the garden, knocking me into a rose bush early in the spring."

"Did I? I beg your pardon." He drew back upon his cigarette, studying the pattern of the smoke as he exhaled it. I watched it as well, before my eyes focused upon that lock of curly hair that was forever misplaced upon his forehead.

"I enjoyed that pub when I attended the university, and it pleases me to venture out without pomp and circumstance. I tend to learn important rumors there, such as the gossip spread by your late-friend's tongue. I had known Marko was scheming against me, but I did not realize to what extent. That one evening proved to be quite valuable."

"I knew nothing," I insisted again.

"I understand that now." The King blew a ring of smoke into the air. "I could see in Marko's eyes that he had never encountered you before. Thank you, Ailana. You have finished your drink and so you are dismissed."

"Thank you, Sir." I rose. Dipping into a curtsy, my wayward tongue continued to speak. "I am sorry your cousin plots against you. I have a cousin who I do not favor, but she would not kill me, nor I her. That I am certain."

"That is because neither of you have a throne."

"We have only a sewing shop," I conceded, which apparently filled the King with mirth.

"Ach, cousins," he chuckled, his dark eyes suddenly erupting with light. "We are nearly two centuries removed from his paternal ancestor, who tied us together in blood. Our relationship is distant and tenuous, but we dance about each other as if we once shared the same womb. Perhaps, we once did in another life. I beg your pardon, Mistress, for I delay you overly long from your own business."

"Oh no, Sir!"

"Oh yes." He waved a hand at the door, where a guard held it open for me to leave. However, before departing, I decided to inform the King that I was in possession of a button from his coat.

"If you should like for me to fix it, I would be most honored, Sir."

"Perhaps, I shall," he replied. "Now, goodnight."

Chapter 13
Dov

My father used to say that we were all one nation now. No longer were we segregated as the people of the motherland, different from those who had solely inhabited this continent before. Since the Great Emperor's time, nearly two centuries past, we were all the same, one blood, one race despite our ancestry.

My mother would smile when my father spoke like this, for she believed it entirely untrue. She would whisper in my ear, "I wish everyone would think the same as him. Unfortunately, it is not so, and you must be wary, my little Dov. Despite your father's words, the others will always look upon you as one of us."

My mother was of the motherland, while my father was of Mishnah. They had met at the university in Turko only a year before my birth. Mama said the attraction was not immediate, for they were strongly different in both their appearances and thoughts. Papa was a dreamer, studying philosophy and pontificating on his every thought, while Mama was practical, studying mathematics.

They met in a school cafeteria where Mama was working to pay for her tuition. Papa had plenty of money to pay for his, as he was descended from a branch of the noble family. In fact, my grandfather was the duke of a tiny province called Kildoo, and

Papa had grown up with much wealth and servants to see to his every need.

However, Papa became smitten by Mama's beauty and her intelligence, which might have been more than his. He chased her all over campus and won her love by taking her to a concert of her favorite band. After which, my grandfather disinherited Papa for his indiscretion.

"Your grandfather is both elderly and foolish," Papa declared, whenever I asked about this family I had never met. "He's a racist and a tyrant. You are better off never knowing him."

Unfortunately, without Papa's trust fund, we lived a pauper's life. Papa was useless when it came to work, for he had never dirtied his hands before. In the past, his former title of Viscount Kildoo had opened doors to whatever he desired and without it, he discovered he was quite lost.

Mama was hardworking and productive, but her degree required more years of study than they could afford. Every day she left before the sun arose to work until the afternoon, when she returned to the university to study until the moons were high. Papa tended the house and looked after me, when he wasn't napping or arguing with the neighbors on the street.

One day shortly after I turned six years old, Mama came home and spoke of people who had disappeared.

"The Duke of Korelesk," she said, referring to a man Papa called his cousin, Marko. "He means to exterminate my people. He means to kill us all. He blames us for the Disease and everything bad that has happened to our planet."

She pulled me on her lap and held me tightly so I would not be afraid of this cousin Marko or what he meant to do. As I leaned against her shoulder, I could feel the trembling in her body and this alone made me more fearful than ever before.

"That's ridiculous," Papa scorned. "We have nothing to fear."

This prompted Mama to shout at him that he was being naive and had always been so. She carried me off to bed, kissing my cheek and telling me not to worry, although by now, I was terrified of I knew not what.

However, the strangest thing happened to me after that. While staring at my ceiling, at the crack that ran across it from door to window, I heard a voice inside the room. In fact, the voice sounded as if it was next to me in the bed. It wasn't that of either Mama or Papa, who were still shouting, banging chairs and smashing dishes on the kitchen floor. They called each other names and Mama wept while Papa swore, prompting the man in the flat above us to bang upon our ceiling.

"Don't be afraid," the voice next to me said. It was soft and sounded like a boy. "I shall be with you. I am waiting for you. It shall be soon. I am here."

"Okay," I replied, seeing no one but my shadow.

Instantly, I felt better, as I knew whoever he was, he was my friend. I could trust him with my life, and I felt as if I always had. Then, I fell asleep that night to the sound of my mama's tears and Papa slamming the door as he went to get a drink from the neighborhood pub.

Mama was right, as she always was, for not long after that, cousin Marko did come for us. His army came to our village, to our building and took all the people of the motherland away.

Mama was at her job, so Papa and I hoped that she was safe, as we peeked from our single window at the street. All our neighbors were lined up, one by one, while the army pointed their guns and shouted commands. The old man who lived three doors away refused to stay where he had been told. Papa covered my eyes when the army shot him with their bullets.

When they came to our door, Papa told them who he was.

"I am Viscount Kildoo," he declared, puffing out his chest. "I am cousin to Duke Marko of Korelesk."

"Prove it," the men laughed, for they did not believe a nobleman could be living in such a dirty place, in a ghetto that was populated by only Mama's people.

"Just a moment," Papa said, as the men pushed themselves into our front room. "I will find something to show you who I am."

He ran to the bedroom he and Mama shared while I stood alone in the front room, staring at the men. Mama had always said I looked like a Korelesk with my fine blond hair and clear blue eyes. I must have, for the men stared back at me and murmured that I was out of place.

"Dov! Come Dov. I need your help, son. Come reach inside this drawer."

"Yes, Papa," I replied, and hurried to his room.

Papa grabbed me as soon as I came through the door. He carried me to the window and opened it wide.

122

"Go on," he pushed me through, "jump down. It isn't nearly as far as it looks. Run to the forest and hide there until this whole thing passes."

I began to protest and struggle in his arms for indeed, the distance to the ground looked quite far to me. Still, he shoved me through until it was only his arms that held me above the ground.

"Goodbye, Dov. If I don't come for you, go to the motherland and be with Mama's people."

Then, he dropped me and I fell three stories. I remembered each moment in the air as if it happened in slow motion. At first, I covered my eyes, but as I realized how slowly this time was passing, I removed my hands and watched the world fly around me.

Papa was leaning out the window with empty arms, and like the building, he grew smaller and smaller until he was no bigger than my thumb. Then, he disappeared inside and I landed upon the grass. Despite the distance I had traveled, I had no injuries. In fact, I felt as if I had flown across the sky upon the giant wings of angel, who set me down with a kiss and a blessing to be well.

Rising to my feet, I glanced around at our now empty building. I could hear the sounds of the army coalescing upon the street in front. A sharp crack filled the air. It was a gunshot, although I didn't know it at the time.

"Run Dov," a voice called me to the forest. "Run away before they come."

It was the same voice, the same boy who had come to my bedroom, my old friend, and so I ran, never once looking back.

For a long time, many days and nights, the changing of the seasons, and the passage of the moons, I lived alone in the woods, wandering from path to path. From forest to meadow, I followed the rivers nearly always by myself. Occasionally, I would meet up with a band of our people, who were hiding from the Korelesk army, just as I. There were many who died there in the woods, having never been exposed to the elements, having spent their entire lives cloistered in the city, never having learned to make a fire.

My friend taught me everything I needed to survive, and I lived, even enjoying the experience a little bit.

One day, I came upon an old man sitting beside the corpse of his wife. She was newly passed and the man refused to leave her.

"We have lost our way," he told me.

Even though I was small, I helped him build her grave. Unfortunately, we had no shovels or anything with which we could use to dig. Instead, we shrouded her in stones, shiny pebbles and granite boulders from the river's edge, until her body was safely hidden from the forest animals.

"What will you do now?" I asked him.

"Wait for my turn to die. I can no more live out here in the forest, than I could become a Korelesk slave. What will you do, little one? How can you manage to survive alone here with winter coming?"

I shrugged and rose to my feet.

"My friend will tell me what I should do."

The old man looked around at the empty meadow and leafless trees, seeing no one, save, a squirrel or two.

"Your friend?" he asked, his eyes twinkling.

"My friend," I repeated. "He has kept me safe this long."

"Then, I suspect he will keep you safe longer still."

Shortly thereafter, my friend guided me to the village at the river's edge. I wintered there in the doorways and beneath the docks. I ate whatever I could find, stealing roots from abandoned kitchen gardens, or bread from window sills, or coins from the pockets of the drunks who lined the streets.

When I met Jan, it was already the spring and I had lived on my own in this manner for nearly a year. I saw her many times upon her boat and at each meeting, my friend would push me in the ribs.

"Speak to her," he said.

"Of what?"

"Befriend her," he said. "Tell her how you love the sea. Go home with her. There is food there for you to eat."

I did as I was told and discovered in the flat next to her own, the very friend that had been speaking to me all along.

I knew who Amyr was and I knew who Amyr had been before. Although I couldn't put it into words, or describe how I came to this knowledge, as soon as I was in his presence, I knew by his side was where I belonged.

When we arrived upon the shores of the motherland, Amyr was taken by the Village Priest and Village Chief, for they recognized in him the same thing that I saw.

"Stay with Pellen," Amyr told me while we were still crossing the ocean in the tiny boat. "Comfort him for he has lost both wife and son."

"What do you mean?" I asked. "You are still here."

"Ach, Dov." My friend sighed in the way that he always had. Then, he nudged me in the arm, a smile playing upon his lips. I could tell that like me, he was glad that we were together again.

I lived with Pellen for more than three years, helping in his shop and attending the village school where I learned the language of the motherland. Little else could hold my attention, for I had grown unaccustomed to sitting in a chair.

I longed to be a warrior, to return to the other continent, and vanquish the army of Korelesk.

Each year, I watched the older boys ride off to the King's village to begin this training, to learn how to fight, and I thought of Amyr, who was already there, preparing for the war we would wage.

"Maybe next year, little Dov," Jan laughed, when I told her of my longing to join those who fought. "When you have grown in height to nearly double, you will be able to carry a sword. Now, it would only drag upon the ground like a dog with a too-long tail. Better you should remain in your lessons and learn how to count all these coins we are earning."

Amyr visited on occasion but as he grew older, those time became rare. His visits were never long, only enough to hear our news.

"And, what of you?" Pellen always asked. "How is your health?"

"I am well, Papa."

"No spells?"

"Not often."

"What of your legs and the weakness in your muscles?"

"No." Amyr would shake his head again. "I am strong because I am here where I belong."

"What of your eyes? How is your sight?"

"It is enough to see what I need to know."

Then, Pellen would nod and insist Jan bring Amyr a bowl of soup. After which, he would begin his inquiries again.

"What do you do? Who teaches you? Where do you live? What do you eat?" Pellen repeated the same questions over and again, although each time, Amyr was as evasive with his answers as before.

My friend would simply act as if he hadn't heard the question, instead asking after our health before begging his leave to go. Pellen would kiss his cheek and with a furrowed brow and concern upon his face, he would watch Amyr until he was too far down the street to be seen.

"What does he learn?" Afterward, Pellen would turn to me, asking the same questions, searching for the answers Amyr refused to give.

Always, I would shrug and pretend I didn't know. But, I did. Amyr learned who he was.

Chapter 14
Rekah

My great-grandfather, who I was named for, was cousin to the Great Emperor. When the Emperor died, the elder Rekah became King of Karupatani for the three decades that remained until his own death. He was very old then, past one hundred ten years, although no one was certain of the exact number, as not even Rekah could remember when he was born.

Rekah bred a large and prolific family, his three wives doing most of the hard work. My grandfather, who at Rekah's death was the eldest of his surviving sons, then followed him to the throne. My cousin succeeded grandfather and when my cousin passed untimely in his youth of the Disease, I inherited the somewhat plain and unobtrusive Karupatani crown and the little house tucked into the woods, my even less obtrusive tiny palace.

We were not pretentious in Karupatani so the title of King meant little beyond this. However, my duties entailed conducting the meetings and councils of the village chiefs, and resolving or at least mitigating the many disputes that arose between them.

I was also to negotiate with my counterpart in the Mishnese Kingdom, to keep the peace, such as it was. During the reign of the Empress Sara and her son,

King Mikal, this was a pleasure, as we were cousins by blood.

Mike had been a good friend of mine. We had both similar interests in sports and drinks, as well as similar strife. Our families had both perished from the Disease that raced across our planet in those times.

Our twice year meetings were times of pleasure that I sincerely missed, for his cousin and successor, Marko Korelesk was not nearly the same upstanding man. Even before Mike passed, Korelesk sought to take the throne, before anyone could think to or respond to deny him this right.

Marko Korelesk would inherit a land in ruins, devastated by the Disease and suffering from turbulent storms and famine. I inherited a land rich with crops and contented people, many of whom had chosen to abandon our traditional ways and venture across the ocean to live a modern life.

From the traders who crossed the ocean and our people who returned, I heard rumors of terrible things happening in the other land. Korelesk was blaming us for all his troubles. My people were becoming enslaved or put to death, but I was powerless to stop him. I had no armies beyond our brave men and horses. Our weapons were only that which we could craft by our own hands, while Korelesk had ships and trucks, guns and lasers, and horrific bombs.

"We have the most important weapon," my younger brother, Ronan, the High Priest, reminded me one evening.

We were together in the Holy Temple, another unobtrusive structure hidden in the woodlands. Despite its appearance, the Temple was a magical place where I could feel the Holy One's presence in my soul. I had come to my brother for guidance, hoping that together we would find a way to save our people across the sea.

"The Holy One has Blessed us," Ronan said, his voice annoyed with my lack of comprehension. "He will send us a means to save our people."

"How do you know this?"

"I believe," my brother smiled beatifically, "and it is also written in the Holy Books."

I believed, but I did not say, that my brother relied overly much on the literary ramblings of our ancestor a millennium ago. However, I could not think of a means myself, so I asked him, "What is this that our Great Father Karukan prophesied? What will save our wayward people from extinction?"

Ronan smiled again.

"If you would read the Books yourself, you would know. Since you are obstinate and refuse, I shall tell you only that you must pray."

"For what? For who?"

My brother shook his head.

I prayed. I did. All the time, for I had no other solution and when the people and the chiefs came to me, I advised them to do the same.

As time passed, I grew skeptical for the refugees' stories became more horrific with no miraculous Intervention in sight.

"Keep praying," Ronan repeated, and though I redoubled my efforts, the doubt in my heart grew. "Patience. The answer will soon be revealed."

I waited and I worried, but ultimately, my brother was right. The answer arrived and it was neither a bomb, or a laser, or a gun. It was a boy, sickly and weak, hardly able to stand of his own accord. He arrived from the coastal village upon a horse, of which he was tied to the saddle so he would not fall.

"Look who I have brought, my king," the Village Chief, my friend, Kirat cried, lifting the boy from the horse and carrying him into my house as if he was a babe. "Our prayers have been answered. The MaKennah, our savior has come again."

For a moment, I had no words to offer in response. Surely, he did not mean that this child would save our people and halt Korelesk.

"This boy?" I said, once Kirat had placed him upon my couch.

The child collapsed against the cushions and closed his eyes, as if he meant to sleep. His breath came hard and his little chest heaved, the bony nobs of his shoulder blades rising and falling through the thin fabric of his shirt.

"Tut tut!" my serving woman cried, appearing at just that moment to see who or what had come. "A blanket, this poor child needs. I'll be right back. Don't you move."

"Yes, this boy," Kirat declared. "Open your eyes, lad. Let the King see who you are."

"Let him rest," the serving woman scolded, returning with a pillow and some bedding. "Now, I'll fetch the young one some good soup. He is far too skinny and in need of nourishment. Afterward, you may talk to him, but until then, the both of you be gone."

My serving woman pushed Kirat, the Chief and me, the King out my front door, as if this house belong to her instead of the man who sat upon the Karupta throne.

Kirat was insistent that this boy was more than he appeared. As we strolled through the village and from there to the Holy Temple in the woods, I remained doubtful.

"What proof do you have that this boy is anything other than a sickly child?"

"He speaks our tongue with fluency although he has never studied a single word. Did you not look at him, my king? Did you not see his face?"

I had, and yes, I would agree that in his features I had seen a resemblance, but in my own face, I saw the same each time I looked into a mirror.

"Behold, my king," Kirat declared, pointing at the frescoed ceiling of the chapel, where the Great Emperor's visage gazed down upon those who came to pray. "Is he not the mirror image? Has he not descended from the Heavens once again? Has he not come to aide us, his chosen people, in the predicament we face?"

"I don't know." I shook my head and with my friend, I knelt to pray. This boy could be merely another cousin begat from another cousin, and descended from one of the sons of the first Rekah's large and extended family. I had many cousins who had left us for the allure of the continent across the sea, so many I didn't even know their names.

When we returned to my home, the child was still sleeping on the sofa, the serving woman watchfully guarding from a chair at his side.

"There is dinner for you in the fridge," she whispered, her knitting needles clicking even louder than her voice, as I came to gaze at the boy's face, to examine it fully. "Now, leave him be! You can bother him when he is well. Go on!" She swatted my arm with a needle and pushed me away.

Kirat laughed, albeit quietly. "It is well you have no summits planned with Marko Korelesk. If you did, you would have to bring that old woman, for surely she is stronger than any general in your army."

"Kari-fa, Kirat," I exclaimed, leading him back through my open door. "Let us dine in the pub tonight for at least there I am treated like a king."

"And, the beer is better than what you keep in your fridge."

The boy continued to rest upon my sofa and the serving woman continued to nurse him with broths and tea, whilst I went about my business as King of Karupatani in my office up the stairs. If I made too much noise coming down the steps, or if I asked, '*What dinner have you prepared for me tonight*,' the old woman would hiss loudly and point a crooked finger at the kitchen.

"He is interesting," Ronan announced the next day after coming to gaze upon this wondrous child himself. "There is a beauty to him that has not been seen since the death of the Great Emperor. What is his name?"

"Kirat said he is called Amyr of Farku, son of the shopkeeper, Pellen and his wife, the seamstress, Ailana."

"Mhm." My brother nodded thoughtfully.

"Do the Holy Books advise us to be watchful for a young Amyr?"

"Indeed," Ronan chortled. "When he is recovered, I will take him in my care, since you seem to be jealous of the attention garnered by the child who is to become your replacement."

"I'm not…" I began to shout, prompting an equally loud "Hush!" from the serving woman, who was still neglecting all duties other than the tending of this young boy.

My brother laughed again, and with a mocking sort of bow, departed through the front door.

As it swung open, I caught a glimpse of the crowd, which had amassed outside, and I heard the voices of the people asking if the boy had awaken.

"Not yet." Ronan raised his arms, blessing the people knelt in prayer.

"This is ridiculous," I mumbled, peeking through my front window. "How many are out there now?"

"A thousand," the serving woman replied.

"Not at all. I count fifty, no, sixty, but no more than that."

"Doesn't matter." She sniffed loudly. "There, there, child. You need to gain your strength." Pulling the blanket up to the boy's chin, she tucked him in tightly, before running a hand across his shiny black hair.

I saw him yawn and he made a noise, a slight cough as he shifted upon the couch. For a fraction of a second, I saw a flickering in his eye.

No. It couldn't have been. It was merely a trick of the light in this room caused by the swinging of the window shades. If not the window, then, the fire had reflected in the boy's eye, for it was cracking brightly from wood too wet to burn. It shot up sparks and flames, even though a moment earlier it had nearly died. Anything else I had seen beyond this, was merely my imagination playing tricks.

That night, I lay in bed tossing and turning unable to sleep. If this boy was truly the MaKennah, our savior returned, what exactly would that mean? The Holy Books had said it would be a time of great strife, and indeed, it was for my people across the sea, but would it be worse than that? Were we at a point once again when our people faced complete and total decimation?

If that wasn't fearful enough, I worried selfishly of my own legacy. Would I, the second Rekah, go down in history as the king who would have let our people die were it not for the boy who would save us from my ineptitude?

I heard a noise outside my door and immediately, reached for my gun. Always, I kept it at my bedpost, just in case. Once, my grandmother, as she slept in this same bed, was awaken by a bear who had wandered up the stairs. Of course, my grandfather had left the front door wide open after a night of celebration and hard drinking. He may have even invited the bear inside, thinking he was a friend.

My grandmother, upon gazing into the upstairs hall, discovered the hulking black form wandering from room to room. Rather than scream or attempt to shoot it, she merely went down the stairs and took the leftover supper from the fridge. Placing it out on the front porch, where undoubtedly the bear could find it, she returned to bed and my drunken grandfather, who remained fast asleep.

I, on the other hand, was now fully cognizant and wide awake. Wearing only my gun, for I slept with nothing else, I opened that same bedroom door to see a form entering my office across the hall. Fearing not a bear, but a would-be assassin, or at least a robber of the King's gold, I followed him, announcing my presence with a shot.

I had meant only to scare the fellow, but he took me by surprise. Where I expected his arm to be, I found instead his chest. This was due to his small, thin stature, for of course, it was the boy who I just killed in haste, which I could only blame on my disorientation due to lack of sleep.

"Kari-fa! I'm sorry." I cried, racing over to the lad as he collapsed upon my floor. Blood spilled quickly, pooling upon the wood, which the serving woman had dutifully cleaned. At first, I tried to staunch the flow by placing my hands upon his chest, but he pushed them away, placing his own hands where mine had been. "I am sorry. I thought you were a bear." I tried to explain as the child coughed and heaved his last breath. Then, he lay silent. "Forgive me, little one. It was a mistake and nothing more. Kari-fa, the serving woman and all the village people will take my crown."

I left him there in a pool of his own blood, but covered by my extra blanket, while resolving to inform my brother, Ronan in the morning. Waking him now would not bring the child back. No amount of prayers or atonement would absolve me of this murder.

Certain that my life was also about to end, I stumbled down the stairs to my kitchen, whereupon I proceeded to empty as many bottles of wine that I could find.

"Ay! Look at you!" the serving woman cried, a few hours later, after discovering my drunken self upon the couch. "What have you done with my little love, Amyr?"

"Killed him," I muttered, although my words were probably too slurred to comprehend.

"Good that the child is finally up. I knew my soup would make him strong. Amyr!" she called, from the bottom of the staircase. "Amyr, come down. I will make for you some eggs."

A moment later, to my great surprise, I heard footsteps slowly treading upon each stair.

"Let me help you, dear heart." The serving woman rushed to the landing.

"No. I've got it," the boy said, clutching the rail, as he took another step.

Now, I rubbed my bleary eyes and tried to focus as best as I could. Indeed, the child was alive and no worse for wear with neither a gunshot, nor a scratch on his body.

Perhaps, it had been a dream. Maybe, my addled brain had imagined the whole event. Clutching my aching head, I ran upstairs to check the bullets in my gun.

Indeed, I was down one and the barrel smelled of lead. In my office, faint traces of blood had dried upon the floor.

Returning to the kitchen where the boy was seated at my table eating fried eggs, I studied him again and once again found no trace of a wound. However, he had been in my office and for what was the question on my mind.

With spoon in the air, he turn to me and for the first time, I saw his eyes, a kaleidoscope of color, every shade in the spectrum of light.

"I was searching for something," he said, responding to the question I had not yet come to ask.

"What, dear heart?" the serving woman cried, running a fond hand across his hair.

"This." The boy reached into his pocket and produced a plain metal dagger with a well-worn hilt wrapped in leather and in need of oil. It fit perfectly in his left hand and the way he held it struck me as one who was accustomed to this weapon.

"Where did you find it?" I demanded, having never seen an ancient blade like this.

"It was in a cupboard," he replied. "Behind the paneling on the back wall." Then, he smiled in a patronizing way.

Briefly, I considered whether or not to demand he return it to me for all items in this house were certainly mine.

"It belongs to me," he proclaimed haughtily, responding to my unasked question, while slipping the dagger back into his pocket.

"Would you like some more eggs, dear?" the serving woman asked.

"Yes, Ma'am." The boy turned to his plate, but not before flashing his brilliant eyes at me.

Chapter 15
Lance

I got turned down for a promotion. After five years as a full commander and after having completed all requirements for the rank of captain, including the multi-species, multi-gender sensitivity training, I applied for command of the S/S Shuttlecock.

Granted, the Shuttlecock wasn't exactly a Class A Battlecruiser like my current stomping ground, the Discovery, but it was respectable ship with a crew of nearly fifty heads. As a supply ship, a cruiser support vessel, it carried a small armory of laser weaponry for defensive purposes only, with two restaurants, one bar, and a small game deck for our entertainment.

"A supply ship is okay," Wen remarked, when I was still contemplating throwing my hat in the ring.

We were in my cabin and Wen was on the floor with Sandy, who was beating him in a game of chess.

How Sandy became such a prolific chess player baffled me, as did most of the things about my daughter. I could barely manage a game of checkers, let alone strategically plan to capture the opposing king fourteen moves before it happened.

"Check," Sandy said, eating Wen's remaining rook with her white queen. "A supply ship is fine, Daddy. Would we be in this sector or another?"

"Phooey!" Wen cried.

"This one." Sitting down at my desk, I studied the Shuttlecock's flight plans once again. I had been stationed in the sector practically my entire SpaceForce career. I would have liked to go somewhere else, to explore another corner of the Milky Way, but this opportunity was too good to pass up.

"Phooey," Wen cried again, as Sandy stood up and came to peer over my shoulder at the screen. That old Imperial coin swung forward and hit me in the back, reminding me how fortunate I had been.

After Sandy had seen the coin and claimed it belonged to her, I took it to a guy in the machining department on board the ship. He put a ring around it so I could mount it from a chain, which she had worn around her neck ever since.

I didn't know why it meant so much to her, why every time I looked at her, that ancient Emperor's profile was hanging over her heart. She touched it constantly too, like a talisman or good luck charm. I figured if it made my teenager happy, who was I to argue? The old Emperor was dead, so what did I care if she loved him more than me?

Frankly, I thought the coin was my good luck charm too, for it had led me from a pretty lousy life back in *The Armpit* on Earth. Now, here I was exploring the galaxy and soon to be commanding a ship of my own. Not to mention, I had my best friends and my amazingly lovely young daughter by my side. I was pretty sure my old man hadn't any clue that I'd reap all these benefits from his gift. Or, maybe, he did. Maybe, the old guy loved me a little bit after all.

"Go for it, Daddy." Sandy patted my shoulder as if she was the parent and I was the kid. "If you want to be a captain, you're going to have to apply for all these postings. Do you want to play again, Wen? I'll let you be white."

"Nope." Wen pulled himself to his feet and stretched his back, rising to his full five foot four inches. "You need to go beat Noodnick now. My ego is so deflated, I'm not sure I can even go to my duty station."

"Oh, Wen," Sandy said with a sigh. "Next time, I'll play without my queen. Will you change ships too if Daddy gets his own command?"

"I guess so," Wen shrugged and headed to the cabin door, "if I want to have any friends. Nobody on this ship likes me except for you two."

"And, Nood," I added. "Although, who could tell."

In all these years of knowing Noodnick, I had yet to hear a word escape his lips.

"His eyes are very expressive though," Sandy always said. "You can look straight into his soul and see what a kind person he is."

Kind or not, Nood was a good crewman and given my druthers, I'd trust him in my engineering bay over anyone else. There were a few others on board I would have liked to steal, but they'd need a powerful incentive to move from a battlecruiser to a supply ship.

As it turned out, I didn't get the Shuttlecock. Politics interfered and I was passed over in favor of a Centipedean, who would become the first SpaceForce captain with eighteen legs.

"Command believes those additional appendages will make him more efficient at handling stock," my commanding officer said. "But, keep trying, Lance. There's a ship out there somewhere with your name on it."

Right. More likely, the eighteen-legged dude was a better fit for the SpaceForce's equal opportunity quotas. At any rate, I did try again a few more times only to be rejected over and over for some obscure reason.

Finally, after nearly a year of applying for every job, I was offered the command a hospital ship on the outskirts of the galaxy. Sandy, like all children, was prohibited from living aboard with me.

"Germs," my commanding officer said. "We can't risk exposing children to unknown space diseases."

"But, it's okay from me to contract the Andromedean eyeball flu or the Black Eye Galaxy's version of the sleeping virus?" I had asked.

"Children are innocent. You signed up for this job, Lance. It's your choice, the ship or your daughter."

"Do you want to go live with your mother for a while?" I asked Sandy, trying to keep the emotion out of my voice. "She's in command of a nice Class A battlecruiser with lots of safety shields."

"Are you trying to get rid of me, Father?" Sandy was sitting cross legged on her bunk, her earbuds destroying whatever remained of her natural hearing.

At the age of fifteen, my daughter was going through her Goth stage, which involved dyeing her beautiful red hair black, except for a few purple streaks. This made a perfect complement to her entirely black wardrobe, her black lipstick, black eyeshadow, and thick black brows. The only color on her entire body, besides her brilliant green eyes and scattering of freckles, was the ancient gold coin which she occasionally wore around her neck. Most of the time, it sat on her bedside table top. Once or twice, I caught her fingering it before swearing at it, or tossing it haphazardly upon the floor.

"Are you dumping me back on her the same way she dumped me on you?"

"No! No!" I insisted, although the thought did cross my mind.

This might be the perfect excuse to send the girl to her mom. Perhaps, female companionship and guidance was what was missing from the child's life, since no matter what I said or did, I was met with disdain.

If I said up, she said down, if I said left, she said right, and if I dared to suggest anything contrary to her opinion on any subject, it was met with a biting comment on my stupidity, or my inability understand.

"It's a stage," Wen informed me, as if he was an authority on teenage girls.

Noodnick nodded, which is about all the dude ever did.

"I'm staying with you," Sandy declared, turning her back to me and cranking the tunes up another notch.

I had no choice but to refuse the hospital ship posting. Sandy dictated my life.

"Uh huh," Wen agreed while Noodnick nodded his head.

"Teenagers." I sighed, waving my hand for another bottle of beer.

We were sitting in a vinyl booth in a bar on spacebase 13-C, and I was lamenting my lack of professional advancement, whereas both Wen and Noodnick were apparently unbothered by the lack of theirs. In fact, the only interest Wen had, at that moment, was the peanut shells scattered across the floor and the snake-like thing that was crawling through them.

"I just want my own ship," I moaned, the beer and my circumstances making me morose. "I want to be called Captain. I want to have the final word."

"Then, you had better quit SpaceForce," Wen replied. "Buy your own ship. Oh, look. It turned around and now, it's heading back this way."

Noodnick, without saying a word, climbed upon the vinyl bench, one beer in his hand, the other in his mouth.

"That's a thought," I thought, having never thought of that before. I could own a merchant trader, or a freightplane for hire. It wouldn't be as honorable as defending the galaxy in a SpaceForce uniform, but I would probably make more money and I could be my own man.

"Now, there's two of them," Wen remarked, joining Noodnick on the bench. "Nope. I'm wrong. I see three, maybe, four."

"My own plane," I murmured. I had a little money saved away for Sandy's college tuition. Probably, there was enough to get a decent ship, something used, a couple decades old. I could use the college money to buy my ship and when the time came, if I still needed to, I could get a loan to pay for the school. I might even get lucky and Sandy would get accepted into the tuition-free SpaceForce Academy. "I'd want something that could handle at least a hundred thousand dead weight."

"Unless we get out of here, we're all going to be dead weight," Wen squeaked as something brushed against my leg, whereupon I joined my friends on the table.

I found an advert on the galaxy wide web, specifically on a site that catered to used spaceplanes.

"What do you think about this one, Sandy?" I asked, holding up my tablet with a series of freightplane pics. It was the right size and the right age, with cabins and bunks for half a dozen crew, and carried enough fuel to travel half a quadrant at lower light speeds. "It's got a large galley and you could have your own cabin with a private head. There's a large common area on the second deck where we can hang a huge vid. We've even got room for a small tender. That'd be cool, right Sandy? It'd be great to have our own ship. I'll name it after you."

"Can I drive it?" Sandy grunted, narrowing her eyes as if my presence was infringing upon her personal space, even though I was standing in the doorway across from her bed.

"The plane or the tender? I think I could probably teach you to fly the tender. I bet that will look good on your SpaceForce Academy application if you already have a junior pilot's license."

Sandy grunted again, which might have meant that she had no intention of applying to the Academy, but because she wanted to fly the tender, she would humor me and pretend that she might.

At any rate, I pursued the freightplane advert, arranging to meet the ship's owner at spacebase 41-B in two weeks, which conveniently coincided with my SpaceForce contract's expiration.

Chapter 16
Rekah

I confessed to my brother, Ronan, of my attempt to kill the boy.

"It was an accident," my brother whispered kindly, as we watched the boy prostrate himself upon the altar in prayer. "In the dim light, you thought him a bear and furthermore, he appears completely unscathed. You see, King-brother, I was correct, wasn't I?"

Begrudgingly, I admitted he probably had been, for while there was convincing evidence that the boy was the MaKennah returned, in the back of my mind, I still held some niggling doubts. True, he had found a knife, hidden in a secret cupboard, and covered in dust that someone had placed there centuries before. And, true his face was a replica of the Great Emperor with eyes that were similar in their oddness, if not color.

Despite this, the boy annoyed me in all he did and said.

How could the MaKennah, the savior of our people be someone that I truly didn't like? Wouldn't his presence glow with goodness? Shouldn't I feel blessed simply because he was around? Yet, I felt like strangling his neck whenever I heard his voice. Sometimes, it was almost as if I had to restrain myself from shooting him again.

"But, why would he come to us in such a weakened state?" I protested to my brother. "And, what of his parents, the shopkeeper and the seamstress?"

My brother shrugged and smiled, as if all the universe's secrets were known to him, but he refused to share them with me, his elder sibling, as well as his lord and king.

"Some mysteries, we are not meant to understand," he replied, as the boy rose from his prayers and came to my brother's side.

I watched him as he walked, slowly and carefully across the chapel floor, grasping each pew with his hands as if to guide him.

"Does he see?" I wondered aloud.

"Does anyone?" the boy replied.

"In theory, no. We are all blind as mice, searching through the dark," my brother agreed.

"You keep him," I snapped, issuing a royal command. "You are well suited to each other. Let you discuss the secrets of the universe and the true meaning of our lives, while I shall go about the business of running this kingdom. Ronan, I proclaim Amyr as your ward and you, his guardian. Good luck to you and fare thee well."

I left the chapel to return to my little house, walking through the streets crowded with my people, who were anxious to see the boy, but who had no interest in viewing me, their true born king.

My brother was exactly the person to take the boy under his wing, for the two of them were much alike. Ronan knew every word in the Holy Books and every other book he had ever read, while the boy seemed to know every word ever uttered by mankind.

"Tut tut, King," my serving woman said, as she put on her cloak and headed to my brother's house. "You sound a bit like you are jealous of that poor sickly, but lovely little lad!" Then, she slammed the door and did not return to make my dinner. Or, any dinner after that. Or, my breakfast. Or, my lunch.

I wasn't jealous, was I? My crown and throne were safe and secure in my two hands. This boy had not come to take them from me, not this weak child.

If he truly was the MaKennah, he would earn it in his own time and in a way that I was powerless to change. Probably, when that time came to pass, I would thank him and bless him for his efforts. I would gladly step aside. At least, I thought I would. I wasn't petty and I wasn't jealous. No, I wasn't. I couldn't be. Jealousy was a childish emotion, and I was not just a king, but a grown man.

I told myself this, although in the back of my mind, wickedness still lurked. Each time the boy stumbled, in my soul, a seed of satisfaction sprouted a leaf. Each time a Village Chief gazed upon him, shaking his head and saying, *'It cannot be,'* the leaf grew a tiny bud that quickly blossomed.

The boy seemed to thrive under the care of my brother and my former serving woman. He grew tall, his muscles thickened, and his complexion glowed with health. After winter passed and the spring arrived, bringing with it warm nights and long, sunlit days, Ronan declared that Amyr was fit to train with the other boys.

"With your permission, King-brother." Ronan bowed, a bit of mockery upon his lips, for I knew he would do exactly as he pleased.

"How can he?" I grumbled. "He is weak and he does not see."

"Our good mountain air and fresh food has cured him of his ailments. He has grown strong and he sees well enough. I will let him. It will be good."

What harm would there be to me if Amyr learned to ride a horse or carry a sword? Again, in the back of my mind, another tiny evil thought lurked. Perhaps, one of our boys would strike him down. Perhaps, one of our own would break his neck, eliminating the question of Amyr and his potential threat to my throne.

Of course, Amyr was not killed during warrior training, or at any other time after that. He continued to grow until he was very nearly a man.

When he was well into his teen years, he stood as tall as my brother and me. His appearance so resembled the both of us, that had I not known any better, I would have thought he was my brother's son.

"I could have said the same to you," Ronan remarked one day, as we stood together at the fence in the village pasture. Amyr was practicing swordplay with a boy of his own age.

Bear was nearly twice the size of him both in height and in girth. Like his father, the blacksmith, Bear was aptly named, for he resembled the large hairy creature which roamed the woods. Bear's head was covered in thick black fur that seemed to bristle at the touch. His chest and back, arms and legs were similarly endowed. Even his voice was low and thick, sounding more like a growl than a man's tongue.

"I think you need to adopt him," my brother continued as Amyr and his horse rushed at Bear.

"Kari-fa!" Bear roared, swiping at Amyr from his left.

"Bear? I don't think the blacksmith would appreciate that."

"You know I speak of Amyr, King-brother. You need to declare him your own son and heir."

"Kari-fa!" Bear roared again, knocking Amyr from his horse.

"Why?" I asked, as Amyr landed awkwardly in the mud. The MaKennah, the first MaKennah was an expert horseman. We all knew that. Surely, this was yet more proof that clumsy Amyr was not our savior after all.

"The people want you to have an heir. They need to know who will be our next king."

"Not Amyr," I began to say, watching as Bear reached out a hand and hefted Amyr back to his feet.

"Brother," Ronan continued. "We do not want a vacant throne for Marko Korelesk to steal. You need a prince, a strong prince to stand behind your back, else Korelesk will believe Karupatani belongs to him."

"Then, I would be better off adopting Bear, for he is clearly the stronger of those two."

"Kari-fa!" Bear screamed for the third time, just as Amyr pulled him from his horse.

Clearly, I had spoken too soon. A moment later, it was Bear upon his back, his thick black hair covered in the mud, while Amyr had a knee pinned against the larger boy's throat.

"Amyr, let him go," Ronan called, slipping across the fence.

"Let him go," I commanded, lest anyone forget that I was actually the king.

I climbed across the fence as well, following my brother through the muddy field, while Bear made bearish noises begging for mercy.

"Amyr, do you not hear me?" Ronan snapped, as he came upon the boys. "Do you not hear the words of King Rekah, your liege lord?"

"I heard," the boy replied, his tongue sharp as if laced with venom. Still, he did not move from Bear, who had ceased to struggle, lest Amyr cut off his breath. "You do not believe I am strong enough to take what is mine?" Then, he turned his odd colored eyes upon me, challenging me to deny the very words I had thought.

"Let him up," I ordered again, for I had conceived of a way for the boy to prove he was worthy of my crown.

With the idea now sprouting like those evil seeds in my mind, I turned on heel and went home, knowing Ronan, like a lost dog, would dutifully follow.

"If he is who you say he is, if you want me to take him as my heir, then he must prove himself worthy to the people of Karupatani."

"How?" My brother hurried to keep pace with me, for I was practically running, so excited was I to have thought of this new plan.

"He will go to the Mishak continent. He will strike fear into the hearts of the people there and he will free our brothers who have been enslaved and bring them home."

Now, my brother stopped and pulled up short, his breath coming hard as he was unused to running.

"Do you mean to send him alone?"

At first, I had thought to, but on second thought, I decided not. Better the boy should learn how to command. Better he should earn the respect of his warriors.

"He may take as many as will follow his lead. When he returns, if he returns, and if he brings at least twenty of our kinsman home, I will declare him the same as my true born son."

I left my brother upon my porch and went into my house, relying upon him to convey this plan to the boy. It was a good plan, I thought, for it would accomplish one of two things. It would either rescue our people and strike a blow for Karupatani, or it would rid me of Amyr altogether.

Chapter 17
Jan

"Where is Dov?" Amyr asked, interrupting my counting.

He had startled me, so much so, I couldn't recall whether I was on one hundred and twenty-eight or one hundred and thirty-nine.

"Amyr!" I scolded with a voice laced with frustration, once again pushing all the coins into a single stack. "How long have you been standing there? I didn't hear you come in."

"You were busy with your accounting," he replied as if that would explain the silence of both door and bell.

"You are a little sneak."

To this he didn't respond, but rather stood blinking, trying his best to focus on my face. Today, in the dim light of Uncle's shop, my cousin's eyes were dark like the clouds in the sky outside. Although I called him little, in his fifteenth year, Amyr towered over me, as he did most men in the village.

"Is it Amyr?" Uncle called from the back room.

"Yes, Uncle. Your prodigal son has returned. Fortunately, he seeks not us, but that monster, Dov."

"Ach, so bitter, Jan," Pellen clucked, emerging with his arms outstretched. "Ignore her, my son. Her unhappiness stems from the inattention of that young fisherman, Torym."

Again, Amyr did not respond save the rapid blinking of his eyes. Even as Uncle rounded the counter and reached up to grasp him about the shoulders, Amyr stood as still as if he had been cast from stone.

"How are you? Are you well? You look as strong as an ox and as sturdy as a ram. Each time I see you, you have grown yet another inch or two. Every day, I thank the Holy One for turning a once sickly child into this healthy young man."

"Thank you, Papa," Amyr responded, leaning his head down so Uncle could kiss him on both cheeks. "I have come for Dov. Will you tell him we must begin our travels before nightfall?"

"Of course. Of course, but tell me to where you will go?"

Amyr named the village up river, the one that was home to the motherland's king.

"I must return," he replied, his eyes shifting to the door.

Uncle looked confused and I could see from his furrowed brow that he wished to ask exactly that which Amyr wouldn't tell. It pained my uncle to know so little of the son, whose life he cherished above all. However, he understood that Amyr's place and purpose was not with us, but with those more important in our land.

"Amyr," Uncle called, just before my cousin disappeared once again. "Be watchful. Whatever it is you are doing, take care. Your head is most valuable when it is still attached to your body."

Amyr smiled and for a brief moment, he looked like the child we all loved. Then, his smiled faded and his face turned hard.

"Do not fear for me, Papa. I shall only do what is necessary to be done. You keep yourself well and look after Jan, for she shall need your comfort."

I didn't know what my cousin meant by that, for I was strong as an ox and healthy from good food and the clean, fresh Karupatani air. I was also extraordinarily happy as my thoughts were consumed by another boy.

Torym was nineteen. He was pale with plain straight hair and a long plain face. From the first time I saw him, I thought Torym the most handsome man in all the motherland and a perfect match for tall, plain, nineteen year old me.

Like my late-father and his, Torym was a fisherman, who each week set out upon the sea. The following, he would return with his holds full of fish. He caught large oily red ones and round fat white ones with enough meat to feed a family for several days. I marveled at these fish, so different from the tiny trout I had chased in the river, and I was awed by the fisherman with the strength to pull them into his boat.

In the morning, before sunrise, on the pretense of walking for my health, I would rise from my cot and hurry to the docks to watch Torym. My heart sailed away with him, although Torym surely didn't know. Not once did he lift his hand in a wave, or cast a smile in my direction.

At night, upon my cot, as I stared at the star-filled sky through our single dirty window, I imagined a life of fishing aboard Torym's boat, the two of us forever side by side. Exhausted, I would lay beside him and listen to his heart beating against my ear, a concert compared to Uncle's heavy snores from across the room.

How Amyr came to know of this was only another of the mysteries locked deeply inside my cousin's head. Even after all these years of living up river in the King's Village, he knew what stirred my heart. What he did with this information, I never would forgive, despite how many years have passed since then.

"Will you return?" Uncle asked, as Amyr stood, his hand paused upon the handle of the door.

Amyr refused to answer, turning away, and dipping his head slightly as if in a bow.

"Goodbye, cousin," I called. "Godspeed. Be safe."

This time, the beribboned bell chimed as Amyr shut the door.

"Godspeed, my son," Uncle whispered, before turning back to me. "Well, Jan, how many coins have we collected today? Business has been brisk. The motherland is good to us. Are you not pleased that we are here?"

That evening, before dusk, Uncle handed me a purse of coins and sent me to the market to purchase our meal.

"Buy yourself a gift, Jan," he insisted. "A pretty necklace or something decorative to wear in your hair. Bring me back a cake or another sweet treat. Tonight, I feel like celebrating our good fortune."

I was never one to turn down a sweet, or a celebration of any sort, so I was pleased to go shopping for our dessert. However, I demurred when it came to my gift. I didn't need such fine things. No amount of feathers, precious rocks, or shiny shells would improve my plain looks. Rather, I should like a new fishing pole, or a net that was woven from green flax.

I wished Uncle goodbye and taking the purse, I walked the short distance to the village market, whereupon I spent the rest of the afternoon lazily browsing among the stalls.

I found nothing of interest upon which to spend my coins, but, shortly before nightfall, as I made to return to Uncle's home, I heard a commotion from behind the market, near the docks. Men were shouting at each other, their voices thick as if laced with drink.

"Foolish drunks," a woman clucked, waggling a finger and showing me a scarf. "Those fishermen are worse than the Mishaks. Lowlife's they are. A disgrace to our people. This would look very pretty around your neck. It is yours for only two coins."

"Thank you, no," I replied, offended for Torym, who was a fisherman of upstanding character and good sense.

I was curious though, a trait that had gotten me into trouble too many times before. Despite my better judgment, I headed toward the commotion instead of home. Torym might be there watching, as his boat had returned today. I imagined myself nonchalantly wandering to his side.

"Ay yah," I'd say with a heavy sigh. "Why do these men act like such fools?"

Torym would respond with something smart and clever. He'd tell me how important it was for men to work instead of drink.

"Lassitude," he'd say, "will be the death of our people."

At this point, I would agree and remind him of my name. I'd tell him how we met once before in the bakery shop. I'd ask how large was his catch this day before telling him of my boat and my own adventures upon the river and how I crossed the great sea with a single sail.

Torym would gaze at me then, recognizing my face and hair, seeing me now with a new found respect.

"Ach, you are the woman," he would say, "who crossed the ocean in that tiny boat. You are quite the sailor. I am humbled by your skill and very impressed." As he smiled at me, his pale eyes would light with surprise, for he was realizing then what I had known all along. "Would you care to see my boat?"

I would take his hand and walk with him to the docks. I wouldn't need his assistance to climb aboard, showing him instead how easily I scaled the nets. Strolling with him about the boat, I would imagine myself with all our sons and daughters about my skirts, casting their own poles, for fishing was in our blood.

Unfortunately, neither my dream nor this conversation ever came to pass. As I rounded the corner of the market, I discovered it was Torym who was making all the noise.

"Take me with you!" Torym was shouting. "I am as good a warrior as any you have before you now. Please! I beg of you. Let me come."

To this, the crowd broke into peals of laughter.

Near the village gates and mounted upon horseback was the Village Chief accompanied by my cousin, Amyr and little Dov. Four others made up their party, boys who must have come from the King's village.

"A fisherman," a boy taunted. "He cannot hold a sword or swing it with our might."

"Your enemies shall be bigger than the salmon who runs from your net," cried another.

"Stay here, young Torym," the Chief ordered. "Your skills are needed to feed this village. You may protect them here if the Mishaks invade our shores."

"No!" Torym begged, causing another wave of laughter to ripple about the crowd.

My heart ached for my love, and I longed to stand by his side. I would tell the village of his strength for great muscles were needed to haul the fish. I opened mouth to do so, the words about to leave my lips, while the Chief and Amyr appeared to confer.

"If you can prove yourself, Torym," the Chief began to say. "We shall let you take a place in our party. Choose any one of these boys and best him however you might."

Now, the crowd gasped and tittered for among the boys it was clear that Dov was the smallest by good measure. Torym stood head and shoulders above my little friend and he was already a fully grown man with arms as thick as Dov's little neck.

"Him!" Torym declared, pointing at the boy. "That little one is not fit to carry my sword."

Dov, who had always been foolhardy, slipped down from the back of his horse. With a broad smile upon his face, he approached Torym in the circle that had formed. Holding up his fists, he began to dance, winding about the fisherman as if he was a snake.

"No, no, no!" the crowd cried. "That is unfair. The boy is too small for you, Torym."

"He has a brave heart," the Chief chuckled. "Go back to your horse, Dov. Torym, pick another closer to your size."

"Kari-fa!" Dov swore. "I want to fight. I can win."

"Him, then." Torym pointed now at Amyr.

"No!" This time it was my voice that shouted in protest. "Not my cousin. His eyesight is very poor."

Torym looked at me, his eyebrows raised briefly in surprise. Then, a smile of recognition spread across his lips.

"All the more reason for me to replace him. What sort of army do we command with a blind man in its midst?"

Amyr nodded at the Chief, before jumping down from his horse, landing unsteadily upon his feet, a hand outstretched. My cousin tripped as he started to rise, prompting both Torym and the crowd to laugh, for little did any know of my cousin's strength.

"No!" I begged again. "Amyr, please don't. You'll be hurt."

My cousin ignored my appeals, slowly approaching Torym, while the crowd grew anxious and excited to watch this show.

Amyr was nearly as tall as his opponent and from his appearance, looked formidable enough, but I was certain that no one understood his lack of vision.

"Please Torym. He doesn't see," I cried, but now my voice was drowned by the cheering of the village people.

Torym's fists were balled up as Dov's had been before. For a moment, Amyr stood uncertainly, as if he wasn't sure what to do. He cocked his head to the side, listening to sounds of Torym's breath and his steps as they approached.

"Come on, fight!" Torym challenged, jabbing him once and then twice in the chest with his fist. Amyr blinked, but did not react in any other way.

"Strike him, you fool," a man yelled.

"Torym, knock him down. We do not need warriors who refuse to defend themselves."

I watched as Torym hit Amyr in the jaw and my cousin fell back upon his heels, his cheek red, his eyes blazing.

After that, I covered my eyes and refused to watch anymore. Instead, I prayed that Amyr wouldn't be hurt. Amyr was no more a warrior than Dov could tend a sheep. Both boys would have been better off working in Uncle's shop.

It was then that I heard a scream and the heavy sound of a body falling. The crowd gasped loudly and someone called Torym's name. Through my fingers I dared to peek, expecting to find my beloved cousin laid low. Already, my feet were moving through the crowd.

"Amyr," I called, tears threatening at my eyes.

"Someone get the doctor," a voice yelled.

"It's too late," another cried.

"Oh Amyr!" I wept. "Let me through! He's my cousin, as close to my heart as a brother."

To my horror, and further surprise, it was not Amyr who was now dead.

It was Torym who was splayed upon the road. Blood was seeping from his eyes and mouth, his skull concaved as if it had been bashed by a fierce hammer. A long gash cut across it where a knife had been drawn.

"One slash," the voices whispered around me as I dropped to my knees before Torym. "The lad killed him with a single stab of his knife."

I did not think my heart could manage another beat, nor another breath would ever fill my lungs. I collapsed alongside Torym, who I had imagined would someday lay beside me in a grave.

The villagers thought me mad, for they had never seen the two of us pass a word, let alone walk hand in hand about the streets. But, Amyr knew my heart. He knew what he promised me years before and he knew what he had taken from me in just this moment.

"Why did you do that?" I wailed and keened as my cousin walked away. "I hate you." I spat upon his shadow and cursed his name.

At first, Amyr didn't respond, nor offer any explanation, until he had mounted his horse and resumed his place among the warrior boys. He gazed at me with his odd eyes, which burned red like the fires of the world below.

"He was not for you," Amyr said. "I have saved you from a lifetime of disappointment."

Now, he smiled slightly, a condescending upturn of his lip, as if I should be grateful, something I never would.

Forever after, I would hate my cousin. Every morning, I would curse his name and never again, would I welcome him to my home.

Another girl, the farmer's daughter joined me in a vigil by Torym's body, until the old men came to collect him and take him to his grave. Together, the girl and I walked behind them to the burial ground. Together, we recited the prayers for Torym's soul.

That night, I lay alone upon my cot, watching the moons rise above the forest trees, listening to Uncle's snoring from across the room. Hate for Amyr, like a tiny cancer, began to grow in the pit of my stomach, filling a void that had once been my hopes and dreams.

Life for me would never be in a boat upon the sea, next to the man and children who I loved. Instead, Amyr had condemned me to remain forever a maiden, tending to this shop. Forever, I was destined to care for the sad, old man across the room.

Chapter 18
Ailana

For a short time, I thought I was in love with the King, not overly so, just a little bit. When I spied him from a distance, or when someone said that he was passing down this hall, or when the guards made us clear away, my heart skipped.

Sometimes, I imagined that when he was on the balcony waving at the crowds, his eyes found me amongst them, and he smiled. From my spot far down below, I imagined he could see me smiling back and mouthing words about his button, which I held tightly in my hand.

"Come collect it," I would say and imagine what we might do on that occasion, for it would entail far more than just my mending.

He was old though, especially to me, who was barely twenty years. He was double my age, or even more so, well into his forties. He was widowed and had lost a child, thus the owner of a shattered heart. Yet, in my innocence and naiveté, I thought myself solely capable of reassembling it.

Certainly, I forgave him for his cruelty to my friend, Lioter. After all, Lioter should never have conspired against a king.

A king was all powerful and entitled to do as his royal heart wished. To that end, if he wished for me to join him in his grand four poster bed, I would have gladly run across the courtyard and climbed the many stairs to his magnificent suite.

Although I had never seen it, I imagined he would have a hearth in his bedroom, which would warm the air to just the right degree. On summer nights, the French doors to his balcony would remain open to let in the fresh ocean breeze. While lying there, I would wear no bed clothes so the air could caress my naked body, and the King would like this. He would smile and his sad eyes would light with desire and appreciation.

Although, he would give me my own suite, the King would prefer if each night I dwelled by his side. While I lay nestled safely within his arms, satisfied in the knowledge that he needed my love, I would gaze out at the white crests of ocean foam beneath the golden moons.

It was just a matter of time. Each day, I fingered his button, assured that this was so. He was only waiting until his heart was ready to love again. It was still too soon since the Queen and his child had passed. When this business with Korelesk had settled down and his reign was no longer challenged, surely, he would announce that his heart now belonged to a Karut seamstress from Farku.

The autumn arrived again and with it, the news of my grandmother's death.

"You must return and help me with the shop," Embo wrote. "I cannot manage it, my husband, and two children all by myself. You must come pay your respect to Grandmother, and say your prayers over her departed soul."

I tore up the letter and pretended it had never come, knowing full and well that my prayers would reach Grandmother's soul from wherever they were uttered.

On the darkest day of the darkest month, when the rain fell incessantly in gray sheets, and the color of the sky matched exactly that of the ocean, a page arrived with a note bidding me attend the King and bring the button that was missing from his favorite cloak.

The Head Seamstress made a tsking noise and muttered something about servant girls acting above their station. I ignored her and cleaned up my table as if I meant never to return. Then, I followed the page across the courtyard to the Big House.

The boy did not take me to the King's office, but rather continued up three flights of the marble staircase to the very suite which I had imagined in my dreams. A guardsman stood at the door, his eyes mocking, a smirk upon his lips, as he held the heavy oak open and waved me through.

The suite was not as I expected, for I had envisioned it filled with light and warmth. Instead, it was as dark and dreary as the shore outside and as cold as the ocean. From what little I could see, the furniture was old and in disrepair, the floors unswept, and the windows splattered with sea salt and grime.

"He's in the bedroom. Attend him there," the pageboy called, as the door shut behind me, muffling the laughter that he and the smirking guardsman surely shared.

Briefly, I thought to clean, as if this mess was entirely my fault. I could hear my late-grandmother's voice admonishing the dirt.

"What man would want to live in a house that was fit for only animals? If you wish to ensnare him, make his home a place that he would desire to be."

To that end, I removed a wayward sock and a shoe from the cushions of the couch. The sock had holes in both heels and toes, and the shoe's sole was worn beyond repair. It saddened me that our king should live little better than the beggars upon the street when once our nation, our planet was the envy of the galaxy.

"*'Tis* a pity indeed," he spoke from behind me, from the door to the bedchamber, and with his words came the stench of alcohol-filled breath. "But, it is not your place to tidy the furniture when I have maids to do this task."

"What maids?" I exclaimed, waving a hand about the room. "It appears that they have been overly long in attending you."

"Have they? Ach, I believe you are correct. I did tell them only come when they are summoned, and I have quite forgotten when I last requested their assistance." He laughed a little at this, clinging to the doorframe where he stood. "No, my wife, my queen would never abide this room in such a state."

I set the sock and shoe down upon the floor, turning to face the King and await my orders. Did he mean for me to repair his cloak, or was I brought here for another reason?

"Neither would my mother," the King continued, strolling across the apartment to a small kitchen area, whereupon he opened the refrigerator. "Or anyone else who has lived in this suite. Did you know, this is the very apartment built by the Great Emperor for his wife? They were the first to share a suite together, followed by my illustrious parents. All of their ghosts live in these walls. This entire palace is filled with ghosts, all of them gazing down at me. All of them reminding me how I have failed in the stewardship of their realm."

The refrigerator door closed, and he emerged again with a bottle of clear liquid in his hand.

"It is a curse to have the blood of glorious ancestors flowing through one's veins. One is expected to be just as great, as if their knowledge has passed to one's brain through their DNA."

"You are a fine king," I said, knowing not how else to respond. "You are doing your best. The circumstances now are extremely trying. You are not responsible for the Disease, nor the famine and poverty that has ensued."

"I do not need you to tell me this," he snapped, bringing the bottle to his lips. "Do you think I do not know how our planet has been rampaged? How my people suffer when there is nothing I can do. Korelesk challenges my every step, yet provides no remedies of his own. And, then there are those who wish to depose all kings and elect a president. I fear I shall be removed in due course for unlike my predecessors, I have overseen the decline of our once great society, rather than the ascent. But, I do not bring you here to garner your pity, or to weep upon your delicate shoulder. Rather, I have summoned you only to repair my cloak, to return the button, so I may go out. The rains have come and soon will be followed by the snow, and I am trapped inside this miserable place like a caged animal."

He paced across the room, waving his hand at the filthy window panes which were rattling from the onslaught of the rain.

"There, there, fix my button."

He pointed at the cloak draped across a corner stand, and so I took it, and sat upon his sofa with my needle and thread. In the meantime, he indulged in his bottle, wiping the spills with the back of his hand, all the while muttering under his breath, cursing the ghosts.

"My wife was better suited for this job, than I. She had a much more level head. Damn the Disease which took her life! Damn Satan for thrusting this plague upon us! Why did he take all whom I loved, and leave me here alone?"

I said nothing, but did my work, letting him rave and rant with abandon. Just as I snipped the thread and rose to present him with his cape, he drained the dregs from the bottom of his bottle.

"Thank you, Miss Ailana of Farku." Instead of taking the cloak, he put his hands upon my shoulders and held me fast. "Ailana of the motherland, whose eyes bespeak the wisdom of our elders, and golden hair mirrors the light of the two moons. Do you know what I want of you now, Mistress?"

I didn't answer, for I suspected, but was too afraid to voice the thought. My heart was pounding so loudly, I feared he could hear it. I had dreamed of this, but now, I wished for nothing of the sort. His breath, strong with the drink, nearly made me retch.

"Come," he ordered, and tossing the cloak upon the floor, he pulled me into the bedchamber, his steps unsteady.

The bedroom was as bad, if not worse, than the rest of the suite, for clothes were strewn about the room, and giant plumes of dust rose as we walked through them. The bed itself was not the elegant and inviting four-poster of my dreams, but rather, a tussled mess of well-worn sheets and wrinkled blankets. They reeked sourly from lack of washing, after hosting sweaty bodies, and they were dusted with cigarette ash.

"No," I said, although my voice was barely that of a whisper.

"Do you know what I do not have?" he cried, overly loudly, clearly drunk and without care. "I have no heir. I leave this land nothing, but an empty throne."

An heir. I thought on this. An heir, a king who could be my son. I could do this. I could provide him with that which he was missing.

Closing my eyes, I ignored his filthy bed, his foul breath and temperament, and I did what I had been brought there to do.

It was neither pleasant, nor unpleasant, merely a task for me to perform. Fortunately, it went quickly and satisfied him well enough, after which, I gladly took my leave. He had no objection as he was quite content, snoring drunkenly, spread out upon the bed.

Two days later, it was announced that King Mikal was deathly ill. The Disease which had taken his wife and daughter before him, was in his blood, and he was suffering a spell. He had retreated to his suite and was attended by physicians who would do their best.

Weeks later, I feared I had contacted the Disease, too, for I did not know how it spread, and neither did I know the symptoms of a quickening in a womb.

For days, although I worked at my sewing desk, my head felt as if it was in a spin. I became clumsy with my stitches and extraordinarily slow in all my work. When it was clear I could no longer manage even the simplest of tasks, the Head Seamstress dismissed me.

With nowhere else to go, I returned to the place of my birth, the tiny corner of Farku, the ghetto filled with those descended from the motherland.

"It is good that you have returned," Embo declared by way of greeting. "You can manage the shop while I tend to my children."

"But, I am ill," I insisted. "I cannot work."

Embo eyed me critically and tapped a foot against the floor.

"You are no more ill than any other woman has been. Who was he, a poor student, or a cavalier professor who didn't know your name?"

"Neither," I mumbled, and stumbled to my old room.

Two weeks later, Embo produced Pellen from the village pawnshop. He brought me a bouquet of roses in many colors, and blushed shyly in my presence. His hands trembled when he touched mine and sweat formed upon his brow.

"He is a good man," Embo proclaimed. "He will take care of you and love you with all his heart."

"I don't love him," I muttered, staring out the window of Embo's kitchen, imagining the King dressed in his heavy cloak, wandering the countryside under this same rain.

"It doesn't matter who you love. You are in need of a man and home. You could do worse than Pellen. He will treat you like a queen even though you don't deserve it. He doesn't know of your condition, so I suggest you complete your courtship at a rapid pace, before it becomes clear that what you carry is not his."

Pellen's looks were nothing, and his conversation was just as plain, but he was kind and brought me flowers at every visit. I grew ill, I thought with the Disease, and would often retch immediately after he left.

"Marry him and move to your own flat!" Embo ordered. "Your malaise is making me ill."

I assumed my days were limited, and grew indifferent to how they would be spent. Within a week, I was married to Pellen, and six months later, instead of dying, I produced a tiny and sickly infant boy.

The Disease didn't take me after all, although it eventually claimed the King, on the same night as the fire's embers flamed bright, and my son nearly died during one of his odd spells.

Chapter 19
Sandy

When I was fifteen, my dad walked away from a non-illustrious career in the SpaceForce. He'd been turned down for several promotions, probably because he wasn't all that great of an officer. He was argumentative and opinionated, filled with ideas that weren't politically correct and happy to argue about them long after everyone else had moved on. In addition, Dad had a chip on his shoulder the size of a battlecruiser because my mom was more successful, having been a captain already for many years.

"What do you think, Sandy?" he asked, showing me a pic of an old freightplane that looked like a deathtrap and was worth more in metal scrap than it ever would have been hauling goods in space.

I responded with some kind of noise, neither happy nor sad, not that Dad would have cared what I thought. He had already made the decision.

I was offered a chance to go live with my mom, even though she hadn't communicated with me beyond a birthday card since she dumped me at the age of eight.

However, we considered it briefly. In fact, Jill and I went on a vacation to Earth and made our best effort to reconnect. Unfortunately, we failed miserably at it.

If I had been given a choice, I would have preferred to have been cut loose, left to wander the galaxy on my own, searching for the place I was supposed to be, because it sure wasn't with either parent.

Ever since my earliest memory, I had always felt like I didn't belong. Maybe, I was a mental case from my mother's inattention, or the lack of paternal figure in my infancy. Or, maybe, I was just a mental case, hearing a voice in my head, who whispered whenever it was quiet, calling to me when I tried to sleep.

When I was ten, Dad showed me an old Imperial coin, and when I first touched it, the whispering voice started to scream. In the back of my brain, an old memory, an old feeling appeared from nowhere.

I knew someone related to this coin, but who it was appeared fuzzy and just out of reach. These sensations both frightened and intrigued me at the same time.

"Sandy's always got some weird thoughts going on in her head," Wen used to say whenever I would zone out during a conversation to listen to the mysterious voice that no one else heard.

Noodnick would nod. He understood. Sometimes, I thought the voice was speaking to him, too.

As I grew older, these confusing sensations abated, for the most part. By the time I was well into my teen years, I decided that I had been nothing more than a totally messed up little kid. There was nothing calming about the coin and it didn't really work with my fashion statement, so I stopped wearing it and found a skull and spiked dog collar to wear instead.

Dad purchased the freightplane from a guy on the Internet, who sent him the door codes and told us to pick it up at Spacebase 41-B. Although, he used all the funds he had saved for my college tuition, I didn't care as I wasn't going to go to college anyway.

"Don't worry, pumpkin," Dad assured me. "Hauling freight, we'll make the money back in spades, and if we don't, you can always go to the SpaceForce Academy for free."

The last thing I wanted was to follow in both Mommy and Daddy's footsteps, so attending the SpaceForce Academy, even for free, would be an option that ranked lower than death. I wasn't about to tell Dad that though as he was stressed and very busy dealing with his new freightplane, *The Flying Mule*, otherwise known as a piece of junk with engines and a cargo bay.

"It's sound…sort of," Wen said, gazing up at the hull. Like Dad, he had resigned his commission, and along with Noodnick, they made up our crew. "It flew here, didn't it? It's got all of its safety equipment on board."

Noodnick nodded, even though he was also rolling his eyes.

"I think it's great," Dad exclaimed. "Now, all we need is some cargo. Let's go up to the bar and see if we can round up some business."

"Aye aye, Captain," Wen cried, knocking his heels together and saluting.

In the meantime, in my head, I heard Noodnick, "What a farce."

I laughed and he smiled because only the two of us were in on this joke.

As Dad and Wen began to walk away, I called after them, "What about me? I'm not exactly old enough to go in the bar."

For a moment, Dad looked confused as if he couldn't quite remember who I was. Then, reaching in his pocket, he pulled out a ten credit note.

"Go get yourself some food and meet us back here in two hours."

So there I was, alone on a spacebase, with money in my pocket. Unfortunately, it wasn't enough to buy me a ticket to anywhere else. Frankly, all I could afford was a chocolate milkshake and large order of French fries.

Having acquired both, I wandered the base, searching for a quiet spot to sit and listen to my music. The arcade and shopping decks were overcrowded with too many creatures and too many smells. All I wanted was to be alone among the stars, rocking out to the tunes blasting in my head, briefly, letting me forget both who and where I was.

I wandered up to the observation deck, only to discover it was blocked off with scaffolding and yellow tape. Not one to be deterred by a *Do Not Enter* sign even though it was written in one hundred and forty-seven languages, I slipped beneath and strolled along the base's topmost deck.

Gazing down at the hordes of people loitering in the shopping mall, I briefly considered what would happen if I climbed upon the rail and took a dive. Not that I would ever really do it, but I wondered.

"You will fly," a voice said.

"What?"

Now, the voice laughed, which irritated me to no end since it was doing so entirely inside my head. I could hear him even though I was wearing my earbuds and my tunes were cranked on high, blocking out all external noise from my surroundings.

"Come here," he called, interrupting a song by one of my favorite bands.

I tried to ignore him, because after all, he was an integral part of my self-diagnosed psychosis. However, he was persistent, calling to me even louder than the bass drumbeat in the song.

"I'm busy," I protested, eating my fries and drinking my shake.

"No, you're not." That obnoxious figment of my imagination broke into hysterical peals of laughter. When he had finished yucking it up, which incidentally, coincided with the end of the song, he very loudly proclaimed in the back of my brain to come hither.

"Where?" I demanded, relenting, because there was only so much fighting I could do with my fabricated demon.

"Up," he said.

"Up?" Up, as in the top of the scaffolding on the very rooftop of this spacebase near the air conditioning vent?

Actually, I wasn't really surprised to see a guy sitting up there. At this point, I was so well into my mental illness, I wouldn't have been surprised to find a gorilla in clown suit, or a donkey sitting on an elephant's back.

Abandoning all reason, what little I had left, as well as the remains of the milkshake and fries, I climbed up the scaffolding's girders as if this was a perfectly natural thing to do. The transit took me about ten minutes, and as I reached hand over hand, rung to rung, it occurred to me I might be suffering from a form of space sickness instead.

Supposedly, I was immune to it, having been raised completely in space, but strange things still happened now and again, and this might have been one of them. I resolved that when I returned home, which I guessed would now be the Flying Mule, I would google everything I could about space sickness and interstellar psychosis in teenagers of human genetics.

"Hello," he said, smiling broadly with straight white teeth and the strangest multi-colored eyes I could ever have imagined.

"Hello." I greeted him as well, trying to perch upon the girder in the same way he did. The metal beams were not only uncomfortable, but icy cold, cutting into the back of my legging-clad thighs.

"Do you know who I am?" he asked as I studied his face, trying to recall if we had ever met.

I'd known a lot of guys over the years, having been raised on two starships and enrolled in the SpaceForce educational system. However, a guy with his wavy black hair and weird eyes, I couldn't recall. Yet, there was something about him that was niggling at the back of my brain, and for some odd reason, that old coin kept coming to mind.

"Nope." I shook my head. "But, you know who I am, apparently."

"I do." Then, he smiled again and I decided, whoever he was, this guy was pretty hot. Probably, he was too hot for a red-headed, freckled, geeky girl from space, even though now I was still in the midst of my Goth phase.

He was strongly built with long limbs and muscles, and his black hair looked a lot more natural than mine. He also had the coolest bird tattoo on the back of his left shoulder.

"I am waiting for you," he said, holding out his hand.

"Why? I'm already here." I held out my hand, but wasn't sure I wanted to touch him.

"I am waiting for you," he repeated, placing his palm against mine. It shocked me like a tiny lightning bolt, which sent a wave of electricity into the middle of my brain.

For a moment, I thought I was going to fall off the girder and into the crowds far below. My heart began to race as my head flooded with vague images, sounds and smells, all familiar, yet forgotten from somewhere else.

"Hey," I gasped, once my eyesight had cleared. "Tell me who you are! What do you want from me?"

Unfortunately, I discovered I was completely alone, at least as far as this girder was concerned. I sat there and took deep breaths, counting to a hundred, until my heart returned to a somewhat normal rhythm. Then, even though my hands were shaking and my knees were weak, I managed to safely climb back down to the floor.

Once my feet were on the ground, I tossed the greasy fries and melted shake into the trash.

"Never again," I decided, "will I eat fast food in space."

"There you are, Sandy." Dad waved as I stepped off the lift, returning to my new home, the Flying Mule.

Noodnick was overseeing pallets of sealed crates as they were loaded into the Mule's freight bay. On the side, in seven languages, the pallets were stamped with 'Cantaloupe' or 'Watermelon'.

"Fruit?" I murmured, coming up beside Nood. "Won't it go bad?"

"Guns," Noodnick replied inside my head, prompting me to wonder if Noodnick was acquainted with black-haired guy who also spoke directly into my mind.

"Sandy, I want you to meet our new navigator," Dad called, pulling me away before Noodnick had a chance to respond. "This is Taul. He knows this sector inside and out. Taul, this is my daughter, Sandy. She's fifteen years old." Dad said this last part with a little chuckle as if to warn Taul against making a pass at me. Not that he would. Taul looked at least twenty-four or twenty-five.

"Sandy?" Taul repeated with his eyes wide open. "Your name is Sandy? But…"

"But what? You've got a problem with that?" I interrupted, tired of guys who apparently knew me from a past life.

"It's short for Cassandra." Dad wrapped his arm around my shoulder, just as the last pallet was loaded aboard. I shrugged him off and glared at the both of them, crossing my arms and daring anyone to violate my personal space.

"I have something for you," Taul said, digging into his knapsack and producing a pair of chess pieces, the black king and white queen from a fancy marble set. "I was asked to bring these to you. He said specifically they are for Sandy."

I took them, and held them in my hand, feeling the marble warm to my touch. On the bottom of each piece, stamped in gold, was the same crest on the backside of Dad's antique Imperial coin. Something stirred in me, a distant memory, an image obscured by fog, voices, sounds and feelings that I knew I didn't want again.

"No, thank you." I handed the chess pieces back to Taul.

"But," Taul insisted. "I brought them all the way from…"

"I said no thanks!" I nearly shouted, as Wen waved from the cockpit door.

"We're ready to go, Captain Lancelot! Time to release this pony from her stall."

"All aboard, crew," Dad ordered, ending the discussion by pushing me up the boarding steps. "Let's take all these fruits to space."

Chapter 20
Ailana

Embo, foolish woman that she was, came back for me instead of escaping into the woods with my husband and our children. Why? I didn't know. I certainly wouldn't have done the same for her.

"We're sisters," she said, even though we weren't. "I would never leave you behind. Get up. We must hurry."

I was still sitting upon the floor where Pellen had left me after carrying my son away to a cruel and certain death. Why didn't he see how much better it would have been to let me be the one to take my child's life? Amyr would have died peacefully, warm in my embrace, leaving from my arms to the afterlife, secure in my love.

"I am not going to the forest," I declared, rising to my feet. The floor was dirty and beneath the sofa was a thick mat of dust and crumbs.

"What are you doing?" Embo shrieked. "Have you gone mad? Sweeping at a time like this, when the Korelesk army is but steps away from our door?"

She rushed at me, while I was taking the broom from the closet, before I had even begun to brush it against the filthy floor. There we stood fighting for it, each of us grasping at the handle, wrestling, and yelling as we did when we were children.

What a sight to see we must have been for the Korelesk army, when they burst through our door moments later. Here were two crazy women battling over a broom, ignoring them completely though they pointed their guns at our chests.

It was only when one man started laughing so raucously, we heard his voice over the noise of our own shouts, that Embo let go of my broom and began to scream in fear.

"Oh, shut up, Embo!" I snapped, now sweeping the floor as if my life depended upon it.

I didn't pay any attention to the men in my living room, as I was already lost in my own world, lost in time and space. When they proclaimed Embo ugly and shot her twice through the head and chest, I thought only of how her blood was making a mess.

Me, they thought beautiful, and me, they decided to use, but I didn't care for my mind was far away. I couldn't have stopped them in any case. A broom handle was no defense against a gun, so compliantly, my body let them, and I lived.

My memories of what happened next were vague, unformed shapes, and distant feelings of coldness, stifling heat, rancorous smells, hunger and thirst. With others in a truck, I was taken from my village in Farku to a camp somewhere in the countryside of Korelesk.

There, I recalled stumbling across frozen ground in shoeless feet. I was washed in a frigid shower, clothed in rags that had belonged to someone else. After which, I was guided to a dorm and a cot, where I sat, preoccupied with my garment's holes.

If I only had a bit of thread, I would have repaired this torn blouse, for the holes were large and though the fabric was thin, it would mend well. Grandmother would never have let me go out in something as poor as this. Grandmother would have snapped at me and thrust a needle in my hand.

"Fix it immediately!" she would have ordered. "Sew them up! No child of mine will go out in public looking like a pauper. Recall that I have a Royal Seal upon my door from the Empress Sara. Neither you nor your cousin Embo will disgrace it in this way. If you do, I shall throw you out upon the street."

"I am already on the street, Grandmother," I replied, following a long line of women to a workroom that was filled with tables and chairs.

Now, once again, I had in my hand that familiar needle and spool of thread.

How long I remained in this place, I could not say, but neither was it much different from my years spent at the Imperial Palace. Each day, I arose and sewed uniforms for Korelesk, and each night, I returned to the hard wooden bunk I shared with another woman.

I aged, and my bones ached. My hair grew thin and I lost three teeth, all of which were in the back so they did not tarnish my once beautiful smile. I grew thinner still, until the rags hung like empty shirts on a drying line. Despite my appearance, somehow, I drew the attention of the Duke, who summoned me one day while surveying the workroom.

He had been standing with our foreman, conversing quietly among themselves, when the foreman raised his hand, his finger clearly pointing at me.

"You," he called. "Come here. Bring your needles and your thread."

I looked about me, and behind me. Surely, I was not the one so singularly designated.

"Are you stupid, Karut?" the foreman taunted. "Or, can you not hear my voice? Choose another, m'lord. That one clearly has no clue."

"No," the Duke replied, his familiar leering smile seeping across his face. "You have said she stitches better than any other. I will have the best, or none at all."

Slowly, hesitantly, I rose from my chair and pocketed my tools. Although, I held no love for the workroom, or the many men's uniforms on my table, at that moment, I would gladly have forfeit this honor to another girl.

The Duke was little changed from the last time we had met. His belly was still large and overbearing, his hair long and thin, and in need of a wash. His eyes were cold and colorless, with no sign of recognition at my face. This calmed me a bit, for though my task may have only been to sew, I feared he meant to use me in the manner he had once professed.

As I followed him to the overseer's building, I glanced quickly around the path, as if I might find a means to escape. If I had crumbs to lay, or a knife to mark upon the foliage, I would have done so. Instead, I searched for a break or a hole in the fence.

Of course, there were none. The fencing was new and patrolled by guards.

"Hurry up, Karut," the Duke snapped. "I have no time for you to sightsee my lovely gardens."

"Yes, m'lord," I mumbled, returning my eyes to the ground and the path beneath my feet.

I was taken to a room, which was little more than a closet with a table of clothing strewn across it. There was a single chair beside it and an uncovered light bulb overhead.

"You have your needles and thread with you?" the Duke confirmed.

"Yes, m'lord." I dipped slightly into a curtsey and waited for permission to examine the goods.

He nodded, waving at the torn lining of a man's black wool coat. Beneath it was a pair of trousers with a large rip in the back seam and a pair of lady's fine silk gloves with a burn in the palm of both hands. These holes were odd, for they were perfectly round and singed in a circle. I guessed them to have been caused by a lit cigarette. Reweaving them would take me more than two days, a task I dreaded for it required patience and considerable skill.

"Can you repair them?" the Duke asked, already lighting up a fresh cigarette.

He blew a ring of smoke into the air of this tiny room, filling it with both his stench and disdain. I pitied the poor lady whose hands had been inside these lovely gloves, for surely, her palms would have suffered the same fate.

"Yes, m'lord. I can fix them, but it shall take me quite some time."

"You have until tomorrow," he declared before departing. "See that you repair everything as if it was brand new."

The door shut behind him, and the lock was turned, trapping me inside to breathe the foul air and dwell upon his words. I grew fearful of what would happen if I failed at this task. For a few moments, my heart raced, and my breath came hard and short in my chest.

For a moment, I thought to scream and to pound upon the door, but who would open it? No one, for all servants would suffer the same fate.

"Calm yourself, Ailana!" I heard Grandmother's voice in the back of my head. "Do what you have always done. Stay alive by the prowess of your thread and needle."

Throughout the night, I sat in that chair, my fingers stitching with rarely a moment's break. The lighting was poor and my back ached, but I did not stop. My stomach growled for I was given nothing, not even the workroom's broth to drink. When my fingers grew sore and bled, I tore cloth from my blouse and wrapped them tightly.

As I worked, my mind wandered far away. I thought of my son, my beloved Amyr, and I imagined him watching over me from the heavens, his soul at peace. If he had lived, he would be fourteen or fifteen years by now. I wasn't sure exactly, for I had no clue how long I had lived in this camp. If by some twist of fate, Pellen had managed to keep my son alive, he would be nearly a grown man.

Setting my sewing down for a moment, I imagined if Amyr lived, if he grew strong, how things might change. In a few years' time, Duke Korelesk would have met his match. In a few years' time, Amyr---Amyr would have been---. A soft tapping at the door interrupted my thoughts.

For a moment, my heart ceased to beat and my breath caught in my throat. I had finished only a single glove, and not even begun the coat and trousers.

"Yes?" I gasped, fearfully. "Come in."

Slowly, the door swung open just a crack, revealing a young girl's face. She was pretty, with a wide clear, gray eyes, and soft chestnut hair that curled around her ears and fell to her shoulders.

"Are you finished?" she asked me.

"Kari-fa!" I swore, as I spied a thin brown mustache above his full red lips. No, this was not a girl at all, but a boy similar to the age my Amyr would have been. He was soft and feminine and as he held out a hand to retrieve a glove, I saw a circular burn mark in the center of his palm.

"Take them with you," he ordered. "Pack everything. We have to leave."

"To where?" I asked, when I found my voice.

The boy looked over his shoulder, to the hallway from whence he came, before turning back to me and whispering so softly, I could barely hear.

"We're going to the Imperial Palace in the Capitol City. The Duke means to declare himself the king. We have conquered all other armies and no one stands to block our way. Hurry up. I will sit with you in the bus, while you finish repairing my other glove."

The next day, I returned to the Capitol City, traveling alongside the boy, who was called Petya. We rode in the servant's bus with the other household staff, and none spoke, save an ancient butler who mumbled unintelligibly under his breath.

Before arriving, I finished both of Petya's gloves, which he wore as soon as I drew the final stitch. Afterward, I repaired his trousers and his coat, but I did not dare to ask him how his clothing came to be so damaged.

At the Imperial Palace, we were assembled in the central courtyard, by the beautiful glass fountain that was built by the Great Emperor for his beloved wife.

"I am the new king," Marko of Korelesk declared, demanding that we all make obeisance before him on our knees.

King Marko spoke more of his plans, but I paid no attention, even though his voice was like a wasp in my ear. Instead, I stared at the fountain, at the brilliant rainbow of colored water, and I dreamed of my son, who would have filled this garden with roses if he was king.

"I hate him," Petya whispered in the midst of the new king's speech. "I hate him. I would kill him in an instant if I could."

"Hush!" I cautioned him. "Do not speak ill of our new lord."

After that, we did not speak another word, for the boy turned his face away.

I continued to stare at the fountain and dream of a day that would never come. In this dream, all the people of this planet would bow before a new king, who had eyes that turned the colors of the rainbow, depending on the light.

The people would love this king, for he would be kind and have a joyous smile, one not unlike my own. The people would say this king reminded them of his ancestor, the Great Emperor, for under his rule, we would prosper once again.

In fact, the people would whisper amongst themselves that it was almost as if the Great Emperor had been reborn, for it was he, the son of his great-grandson, Mikal, who was the last to descend from the Imperial Blood. As for the new king's mother, well, she would be quite content standing by his side as he reigned upon the Imperial Throne, for that woman was none other than a poor, Karut seamstress, me.

Chapter 21
Dov

I decided I hated the sea. After our last voyage in Jan's tiny boat, I had vowed never again to sail across the ocean. I had no need to return to the other continent. I had no desire to reclaim my familial duchy of Kildoo, and frankly, I enjoyed living in the motherland, so I figured there would never be a reason I should have to travel again.

I was wrong. Amyr came and bid me pack my few belongings, as well as find a horse for our trek back to the King's village.

"I don't have a horse," I said, to which he just gazed at me with his strangely colored eyes. "I guess I'll have to find one."

"I guess you will," he repeated. "And, do it quickly. We ride at nightfall."

I went to the Farmer Lehot, who had always been kind to me, especially when he had caught me stealing raspberries from his bushes, or apples from his trees. Instead of grabbing my ear and dragging me to the Village Chief for punishment, he would make me pick the ripe berries until my hands bled from all the scratches.

Farmer Lehot had a daughter, Lorinda, who was just my age, which was why I liked to spend so much time around his orchard. Purposely, I'd steal an apple, just to earn the chance to perch in one of his trees where I could watch Lorinda churning butter on their porch.

Lorinda was tiny, even smaller than me, with long, dark thick hair that was perfectly straight without a single curl. When she moved it was as if every hair followed her in tandem. I loved to walk behind her watching this dark, silky curtain swing from side to side, imagining what it would feel like in my hands.

If her hair wasn't beautiful enough, Lorinda's eyes were like two limpid pools of mud, the kind that would swallow you up in just one step. They were framed by long thick lashes in the same color as her hair, and her red mouth was always open in a circle.

The only part of Lorinda that wasn't absolutely perfect was her left front tooth, which instead of pointing down, stuck out at an angle. I used to imagine what it would feel like to kiss those sweet round lips, to feel that tooth poking through the delicious softness, bumping my tongue.

On the other side of the orchard, Farmer Lehot had some pasture land where he kept his goats and sheep, as well as several horses to pull his carts. Lorinda had a pony and when she wasn't doing her chores, invariably she was upon that pony's back.

It might have been the heat or dehydration that made me so whimsical in those late summer days, but as I sat in the trees picking fruit, I dreamed of the two of us on the pony galloping away. We were both so small and the pony fat, he could have easily carried us together, or so I thought. Imagining Lorinda pressed against me in a saddle nearly felled me from a tree.

Now, when I needed a horse, my first thought went to Farmer Lehot. I would go ask him if by chance, I could borrow a steed for just a few days.

"I'm off to the King's Village," I would declare. "No, I don't know when I shall return, or if I ever will, for I have been chosen to become a warrior to fight the Mishaks."

Undoubtedly, Lorinda would hear this and come running to my side from wherever she was. She might have been in the barn and there might be pieces of hay stuck in her hair.

"Take my pony," she'd insist. "I'll ride with you so I can bring him back."

Then, the two of us would travel to the King's Village in the same saddle just as I had dreamed.

"Dov!" Amyr snapped, still staring at me. "Hurry up."

"Yes, Amyr," I mumbled, heat searing like a burn across my face.

I ran to the farmer's house and presented my case to borrow a horse, while waiting for Lorinda to magically appear. Unfortunately, she was at the market selling boxes of fruit and berries from her stall. Her pony was in the back pasture, and I could see now he was obviously too small to carry two.

"You'll take one of my old draft horses," the farmer insisted. "I'll arrange to have him returned to me. Bless you, little Dov. You're a brave young fellow."

So, there I was astride this enormous furry beast, while all of the other warriors rode sleek and fast fighting steeds.

"Don't pay any attention to them," Amyr whispered when the other boys laughed at my ancient mount.

I wouldn't have, but they laughed again when Torym, the fisherman, challenged me to fight. I knew that would have been a losing proposition for me, and had Lorinda not emerged from the market to watch the show, I never would have slid down from the back of that horse.

As it turned out, I didn't have to fight anything except the urge to take the horse and disappear, after Amyr killed the fisherman with a single blow from his blade.

"Why did you do that?" I asked him later, during the trip to the King's Village, as we rode side by side, and alone at the back of the pack. "He was a decent fellow. Nothing was bad about the fisherman, Torym."

"It was necessary," Amyr murmured. "Sometimes I must act even when it doesn't appear to make sense."

"But, why did you let him hit you, if you meant to kill him anyway?"

Amyr snorted. "It is my strategy. You ought to learn this since you are so very small. If they think they can best me, they let down their guard. Furthermore, it absolves me of any guilt when I take them out."

I didn't think Amyr ever felt guilt, nor remorse in this life, or any other. I did, though. My heart was soft, not a stone like his, and kept replaying the whole event over and over in my mind.

As Amyr swung his knife at Torym, I saw Lorinda approach from the corner stall, her mouth open, her protruding front tooth, a tiny speck of white.

Amyr's hand and blade connected with Torym's head, followed by the sound of bone crunching. Lorinda screamed the fisherman's name, before fainting. She fell over like a rock, her body thudding as it hit the wooden boards, her head knocking against the neighboring stall, before she passed out.

My instinct was to jump down from my horse again, and run to her side, rescue my love, but Amyr was already mounted and demanding we move out.

"Get going," he ordered me, leaving me no choice but to follow,to obey his command, for I was his squire, forever his servant, and his eyes and ears.

After two days of travel, dirty and wet from the rain, as well as hungry from lack of food, we arrived in the King's Village. Not five minutes later, I was told we must board a boat. I wanted to protest, but my opinions were neither asked for, nor desired. Despite my reluctance, in a matter of moments, I was once again upon the waves.

At least this time, the vessel was fairly large and I could stand on the deck and heave my sickness into the sea. The wind was cold and it helped to calm my stomach a little bit.

"Come below, Dov." The boy called Bear waved to me. "You must learn of our mission and be marked."

Mission? Marking? I didn't want either of these things. I wanted only to go home to Lorinda, who I now realized, had fainted at the death of another man.

I didn't jump off the boat, or swim back to the shore. Instead, like a good soldier, I followed Bear down below into a room that was hot and filled with odors that alone would have made me sick.

"Ay yah, Dov!" Amyr waved, an odd smelling cigarette perched precariously upon his lip. Like everyone else, he was naked above the waist, while Pori worked intently, drawing something upon his back. "What do you think it is?" Amyr slurred, the cigarette obviously more than just tobacco leaves. My friend had certainly changed in the King's Village, and I wasn't certain it was for the better.

"It's an eagle, Amyr," I muttered, noting the newly inked black wings that spread across his shoulders, recalling a similar marking at another time, although I couldn't say exactly where or when.

"Ay yah, of course," Amyr laughed drunkenly, his eyes flashing in a million colors all at once. "What else would I be? I am the same as I have always been."

"You are next, Dov," Pori murmured, waving a needle in my direction. "What creature owns your soul? Every warrior of Karupatani must be branded with their animal spirit."

The only creature that came to mind was a woman, or to be specific, Lorinda, for every waking and sleeping moment, my thoughts were entirely upon her.

Amyr made a huffing noise.

"Dov," he shook his head, "that one was not for you. You will thank me later, as will Jan. Ach, what I must do on your behalf."

"What are you, little Dov?" Bear called, perched on a bunk. "Something small. Something light of weight, yet something that flits about. I know! You are a hummingbird."

"I am not!" I protested. "I am not anything at all."

"Maybe, a rabbit," Borak snickered. "The type that likes to run and hide in holes."

"Or, a goat," his brother, Turak called from across the room. Before him were stacked many empty bottles of ale, as well as a pile of butts and ash from dozens of cigarettes.

"Dov is the phoenix," Amyr announced, rising to his feet and stretching out his back. The great black eagle quivered, looking fiercer than it did when he was still. It was a good rendition, though. Pori was quite the talented artist. "Come now, Pori. Put a phoenix upon Dov's arm, for he shall rise from the ashes once again."

A phoenix. I liked that. It, too, was a great and noble bird. Although, I didn't desire any marking, if I had to have one, this could be it.

I removed my shirt and let Pori create, although the swaying, hot room made my head spin and the scent of old smoke and ale-laced breath sent my stomach lurching. As soon as the rendering was finished, I lurched up the stairs, before I spewed all over everyone.

That night, I spent up on the deck as I had all the ones before. There I sat on a box filled with ropes and floats, and wrapped in a blanket I had stolen from a berth below.

The sea was calm and the air was warm, when Amyr sat down beside me and lit a cigarette. I watched him flick a finger and from nowhere fire appeared. He drew long and hard on the smoke and then, like a dragon blew it all into the air. How he had changed from the sickly, weakened youth to this man who was hard and cold as steel!

"We land in Farku tomorrow," he said, his face turned up to the morning sun, his eyes alight with a thousand colors, before they turned a dark and angry red. "We will set fire to the land, to the buildings, and all who dwell within, and then, you will rise from the ashes like your spirit bird once again."

"Me? Not me. You. You are the one, the MaKennah who has returned."

"Not I, Dov. Not this time. Now, I am merely Amyr, son of Pellen, shopkeeper from the Karut ghetto in Farku, and Ailana, seamstress to the King. You are the phoenix, the firesetter. You are the one who will command. By birthright, the throne is yours for you are the sole grandson of the Duke of Kildoo."

Chapter 22
Ailana

Once arrived at the Imperial Palace and settled into another tiny room in the servant's wing, this time with a bed solely for myself, I was summoned to the Lord Chamberlain's office. There, I was declared the Royal Head Seamstress and given a key to an empty room to use as my shop.

It was, in fact, the same room, the same desk, the same needles and threads, and the very same table where I had worked once before. Long ago, it seemed, nearly a lifetime in another world, I had sat at this same window mending and sewing.

That was when I still had hopes and dreams that might someday come true, when I had coins in my pockets, and fine department store dresses to wear. That was also when a handsome noble man met me by the fountain and shared with me his soul, and later, I shared with him my body.

Now, every day, I stared out at the frozen courtyard, for the winter had come and was vicious, punishing us with heavy snow. The gardens were nothing but skeletons of dead shrubs, and the rose bushes were empty and layered in ice.

I never left the servant's building even to walk about, so did not see how the ocean had breached the seawall on the palace's eastern shore. A maid, who cleaned the apartments of the nobility, told me that all the sand had eroded until there was none. All that remained was a wall of large, black boulders and the frigid waters splashing upon them. Angry, bitter ocean tears were cast upon the windows, no matter how high above they were.

"It is because the angels are angry," the maid whispered. "They do not approve of our new king."

She was bringing me her thin coat with a torn lining and sleeves which required the filthy lace to be replaced. Like most, she had no coins to pay me. Instead, she offered me a half loaf of bread, or four chocolate cookies uneaten by the King.

"Why do they not like him?" I asked, accepting her gifts and stowing them in the closet beneath an overturned box.

"He is cruel," the maid replied, her hand paused on the door. Then, she bit her lip to keep from saying what all knew. Marko Korelesk had stolen the Crown, even though it had been empty, awaiting a new head. "They say-they say-there is another to whom it rightly belongs."

"What is he called?" I feigned disinterest, although the needle between my fingers began to shake. There was one. Only one, if he still lived, by birthright it belonged to him.

"A boy." She spoke beneath her breath, coming closer as if to watch my needlework. "A Karut boy."

Her foul scent seeped over my shoulder, for this poor girl knew not to wash or brush her teeth. Though, this stench bothered my nose, I resolved to bear it so I might hear.

"Who?" I asked again, waiting for the name, which I had granted him myself and held closely in my heart every moment of every day. "Who told you this? Who else knows of this boy?"

"I overheard a conversation between the Lord Chief of Staff and a man who came into his office. I was in the corridor dusting and could not help but overhear their words. The man said there is a boy. A boy who the Karuts claim is the MaKennah returned. This boy's face, they say, resembles that of King Mikal, and the Great Emperor before him from long ago."

My heart raced a little, although this gossip was not a confirmation. Mikal favored his Karupta ancestors and that family was large and filled with many boys. Grandmother often said that we, too, were descended from those same genes. Only one boy, though, only one would have a feature that set him apart.

"What of his eyes?" I whispered, attempting to make a stitch. I was so distracted and anxious that my needle moved astray and like a novice, I stabbed into my thumb instead.

"Foolish girl!" Grandmother yelled from the recesses of my brain. "Concentrate on your work or you will die alone in the snow."

"His eyes?" the maid repeated. "How did you know of the boy's strange eyes?"

"Tell me!" I demanded, brandishing my needle like a sword.

The girl looked at me with curiosity, biting her lip and debating whether or not I had gone mad.

"He said---." She opened her mouth but was interrupted by the swinging of the door. The wind grabbed it and slammed it open, allowing a gust of frigid air to enter the room. "I'll return tomorrow, Mistress Seamstress."

The maid's footsteps quickly ran away. I ignored her as if she was no one, listening to the soft sounds of another as he approached on shoes too thin to tread through the mountains of ice and snow lining the pathway to my shop.

"Ailana," the voice said, too high and too soft for such a boy. "Will you fix something for me quickly? I'll pay you double, or even triple for your time."

"Of course, Petya, and you owe me nothing. Your sweet company gives me pleasure enough." I set down the maid's torn coat and took his socks, which needed darning in three places. "Are you hungry? I have bread and cookies. Please eat them before the mice."

The boy shook his head and sat in his usual chair. He had grown tall, but his limbs were far too thin. The faint mustache, which graced his lip, had darkened, but was out of place upon a face that looked more like it belonged to a woman.

Still, we went through this routine on every visit, for he came often with his clothes always in need of repairs. He spent hours by my side, sharing gossip and trading news, and I enjoyed his company for he was just my Amyr's age.

But, Petya's life was hard and filled with a pain of which I dared not to think, or question. What was done to this boy, when he was not with me, burned a hole in my soul and the pit of my stomach. Instead, I sought to humor him, to make him laugh, and smile, to forget his woes. I wished that far off in Karupatani, a woman was doing the same for my son, for now I knew with certainty that my Amyr was alive.

"You're not eating enough," I scolded, followed by a chorus of motherly clucks, while laying the cookies in front of him on my only silver tray. "How are you, dear? Tell me your news. Are you feeling better? Did you get over your ague and malaise?"

Petya turned his gaze to the window, to the ever present snow that never ceased to drift from the sky. His eyes grew wet, sending a spike of fear through my heart. I turned my own eyes away, examining the socks and putting a finger through each hole.

"My son would destroy a pair of socks each time he wore them. Do you think far off in the motherland, there is woman to repair his, while he sits beside her in a chair?"

"You said your son was dead," Petya murmured, his voice empty of emotion.

"I don't know. I hope not. I heard---I heard, just this day---"

"I hate him," Petya interrupted, his voice suddenly growing violent. "I would kill him if I could. I would slash his throat and watch him bleed."

Not my son. I knew he did not speak of my son.

"Hush now," I implored him. "Don't say such evil words. The Evil One will hear you and bid you come to serve him."

Petya shook his head.

"I don't care. I would serve him for he is kinder than my current master."

To this I didn't respond, for I had no words of wisdom I could share. Instead, I picked up my needle and prepared to begin my mending. I noted the perfectly round hole upon the sole where the threads of wool were once again singed.

"Do you need some salve, Petya?" I asked, keeping my voice steady and without pity, for the boy would only snap at me if I treated him like a babe.

He didn't answer, and when I looked up from my needle and thread, I saw tears drifting quietly down his cheeks.

How I wanted to take him in my arms, to hug him and to comfort him! How I wished I could make his demons go away. Yet, in the past, when I touched his arms, he would forcefully push me aside.

"I do not need a mother," he would snap. "I am not your replacement son."

Petya left immediately after that, refusing my salve, or the handkerchief to dry his tears. From my window, I watched him disappear, like a ghost in the wilderness of snow. As I held his ruined sock in my hand, I decided the maid had been correct. The angels were angry and they were punishing us for allowing such an evil king.

I repaired Petya's socks, but he never came to fetch them. In fact, for a week, he was unseen about the palace.

"Everyone is searching for him," the maid whispered when she arrived to collect her coat. "The King is in a rage and demands the boy be produced forthwith."

I worried after Petya, for he had become my replacement son. As to the king's interest in him, that I did not question, nor did I doubt the King was behind the boy's disappearance.

For this and more, I despised Marko Korelesk. I called him a pretender to the throne and I did not care who heard me speak these words.

Ten days from the day Petya left me with his socks, when the snow had abated for a few hours, a guard spied a body upon the rocks below the seawall. It was frozen and blue, but his form remained intact.

Immediately, he was recognized as Petya. Whether he jumped himself, or was pushed into the waters, was still in doubt. To me, it didn't matter, for I knew who killed him, if not by his own hand.

"Careful, Mistress Seamstress," the maid said. "If His Majesty hears of your disdain, you'll be sent out upon the streets to join the beggars in the snow."

"I don't care," I declared and though a great injustice had been done, I took comfort in knowing even a king wouldn't escape God's Final Judgement.

The following day, a funeral was held for Petya, in which he was entombed in the mausoleum adjacent to the palace. Curiously, this boy was placed in building full of noble souls, surrounded on either side by the ducal ancestors of Korelesk.

There were few who attended this simple service beyond a maid, four page boys of Petya's age, an elderly butler, a young uniformed guardsman, and lastly, me.

"A pity," everyone said, placing a hand upon the polished stone, wishing the child peace in the next world and whatever came beyond. Then, they walked away, except for the guardsman, who like me chose to sit upon a bench and reflect.

"I shall miss him greatly," the young man said.

"As will I. He was far too young to die."

No more words passed between us until much later, when the sky grew dark and the building chilled as night began to fall.

I would have stayed until dawn, if I could have. It was the custom of my people to sit beside the dead until they were well upon their way.

Although Petya was not of Karupatani, I felt it was something that I must do. The young guardsman seemed inclined to do the same, until our vigil was interrupted by an angry voice.

"What in the hell are you doing here?" the King demanded, interrupting our silent contemplations.

"I---" I rose from the bench and began to speak, assuming that his words had been directed at me.

"I told you to stay away from him! Now, you disobey me even in his death! Be gone with you, or you shall follow him across the seawall into the surf."

Before I could speak again, the guardsman quit the room, running quickly past the King, while I stood trembling in my place. My own knees were too weak to move, and my heart was fluttering wildly in my chest, as the King took the guardsman's seat upon the bench and sat down heavily.

I thought he would order me away, as well. At least, I assumed he would question who I was. Surprisingly, Marko Korelesk ignored me. Burying his head in his hands, the King began to weep, leaving me to watch his sorrow in stunned amazement.

"I loved him," the King sobbed, as great tears rolled down his cheeks and I, who should have held her foolish tongue, lashed out with angry words.

"Love?" I spat. "That is what you call what you have done to him? His death is on your shoulders, for if not by your own hand, you certainly drove him to it."

"What?" The King looked up and as if realizing I was there, he narrowed his red rimmed eyes and pointed at the floor.

Hesitantly, for I had vowed never to make obeisance before him again, I stood my ground. Crossing my arms before my chest, I refused to kneel.

"I said, you killed him," I accused. "If you truly loved him, you would have seen the pain you caused. It was plainly evident if you had dared to look. Your actions with him were despicable and repulsive. No amount of penance will absolve you of this sin."

"Then, you are mistaken, Mistress," the King replied, his voice going hard and cold. "I neither wished for him, nor caused him pain. I sought only to provide him with a life of honor and respect. It was his own poor choices which hastened his death."

Now, it was I who gasped and cried aloud.

"What? Honor and respect, Sir? After what you did to him? How many times did you use him as you once said you would use a colt?"

The King shook his head and his brow furrowed as if trying to recall.

"In my presence, you admitted such an affinity," I declared. "Before, your cousin, King Mikal, in his office, many years ago."

"You think I did what?" Now, the King's voice rose as a spark of recognition flickered through his eyes. "You are presumptuous, Mistress, and quite mistaken. Who do you think you are that you can accuse me of such a heinous act at the graveside of my only and beloved son?"

"Son?"

Had I been mistaken? How did I not know there lived this prince?

"Petya?" I whispered. Aye, Petya Korelesk. Petya, the son of the Duke with the same clear gray, almost colorless eyes.

Now, I did drop to my knees and I bowed my head, as tears fell from my eyes. I had been wrong. I erred horribly.

"Forgive me, Sir," I begged. "I knew not of whom he spoke."

"What did he tell you?" the King demanded, and when I could not speak, for my throat was thick, he put his hand upon my shoulder and bid me sit beside him on the bench.

We sat as this, side by side, for many hours, until the dawn broke and the sky began to lighten. Outside the snow had ceased to fall, although the ground was thick with mountainous drifts.

"Ride with me, Mistress Seamstress," the King said, his voice hoarse from hours of weeping and so I was returned to my workshop in the Servant's Wing by the warmth of the King's own sled.

During the springtime, I acquired a friend. He was an elderly gentleman who had once been in the Imperial SpaceNavy during the last days of Empress Sara's reign. Despite his advanced age, Kenan worked in the Big House opening and shutting the main door.

"Once, my task was done automatically. During Sara's time, there was an abundance of energy to do these things."

"My grandmother spoke of sewing machines," I agreed. "They would do my task in a minute instead of the hours I spend stitching by hand. In the evening, there would be no need to put salve upon one's fingers."

"Ach, those were the good old days," Kenan said and sighed. "But, that is what every old one says. Why, in my youth, I recall my grandfather saying the same. You are doing a fine job on my shirt, Ailana. No machine could stitch finer than you." Kenan's eyes sparkled, inviting me to smile and blush a little. "You have the loveliest smile, Mistress Seamstress. It is a joy to gaze upon your face."

"Is that why you visit so often?"

"That, and my preponderance to snag my clothes upon every nook. But, I confess, I enjoy your company much more so than any other."

Kenan asked me to walk about the gardens with him when I closed my workshop for the night. Spring had arrived and with it the longer days. The weak sun slowly melted all the snow, sending rivulets from the palace down the hills, leaving the courtyard clean and green with fresh, new growth.

At first, I demurred to Kenan's request. I did not desire such a friend, or a new love. My heart was heavy from loss and Kenan was old, and would not remain with me for very long.

Here was I, once surrounded by family at every turn, and now, I saw them only in the darkness in my dreams. Every night, I saw visions of my son, tall and strong, fully grown, but with Petya's face.

"Amyr!" I would call to him, my arms outstretched, my eyes thick with tears.

"I am not Amyr," he would reply. "I am another. I am your son."

"Will you come, Mistress Seamstress?" Kenan stood by the door and held out his hand. Like the gentleman he was, he bowed his head in way reminiscent of the days before.

"Go on!" Grandmother's voice spoke up from the corner of my brain. "Why not? You could do worse than this old man. He will care for you and keep you safe until he dies."

Sometimes, I wished I could speak back to Grandmother and remind her that even death had not removed her stewardship over me. Instead, I said, "Why not?" and found my sweater, locked my door, and took a turn about the courtyard by Kenan's side.

We took to walking about nearly every evening, as spring became summer, and the nights grew long. Our friendship grew as well, and I began to care for him, despite my reluctance to share my heart.

"Marry me," Kenan asked. "I would spend the final years of my life waking up to your smile."

I couldn't and though, I thought long and hard, tempted by the comfort of his quiet, steady presence, I did not know whether my husband, Pellen had lived or died.

"I can't," I insisted. "However, I will live with you as man and wife."

Thus, for a short time, we shared a bed and though his lovemaking was no better than Pellen's had been, it was a comfort to be held by a man. I did not fear that inside me a baby would quicken, for I was already in my fortieth year, and Kenan was so old, surely he had nothing left to sire one.

However, our time together was brief, ending quickly, but not by death. Instead, one day, I was summoned to the Big House by a guard, in the same manner as once before.

"Come quickly, Mistress Seamstress," he said, so I took my sewing kit with needle and thread, assuming a repair was required at the behest of our new king.

I passed Kenan at the doorway. He raised his eyebrows in surprise, as I was guided by the guard up the staircase to the topmost floor. There, I was instructed to wait outside a door. It was the self-same door, the one I had been to once before. I feared that my summons were again for the self-same purpose.

The guard knocked and backed away, a snicker upon his lips and a leer in his eyes, before removing himself to the corner, whereupon he stood, watching me with pleasure.

Presently, the heavy door swung open.

"Ah, Mistress Seamstress," the King declared. "I have need of your skills. Do come in."

"Yes, Sir." I curtseyed dutifully, although my heart began to race. I held my sewing kit before me. "What would you like me to repair?"

"Ha!" the King chortled, and like his cousin, King Mikal before him, he emitted a foul gust of alcohol-laden breath. "My heart, Mistress. It is broken and in need of mending. I can see you possess this skill, for I have been watching you these many months, wondering where it was that I first spied your lovely smile."

"I don't understand, Sir," I protested, refusing to enter the chamber, though he beckoned me in.

"Come, woman. Step inside. I do not wish to provide more entertainment for the guards than they deserve."

What choice did I have? To run from the King and be shot by the guard, who sneered as if he was already enjoying the show? To die now would be such a cruel twist of fate, for I had reached a state of contentment, a peace with Kenan that I had never known before.

"Go inside," Grandmother advised. "There is yet more which you must do. You have a son who needs you. For him, you must live."

I went in and I sat upon the couch, waiting for what surely would come to pass. As I suspected, the needle and thread were never taken from the kit.

"You are a servant," he cried, when he had done what he wished to do. "You are a Karut woman of no-account, yet you draw my eyes whenever you are near. I have watched you walk about the courtyard. I grow jealous when that old man goes inside your door. My cousin used you, and so shall I do the same.

"How come you, foolish woman? What is it about that you that you have captured the heart of two kings? Your smile is beautiful and it slays me as if I was a senseless boy."

I had no answer, no explanation, for I was just as confused myself. However, in my heart, a seedling of a thought began to grow.

There was another man for whom this throne was destined, another who deserved it by virtue of his birth. He was a man who would love me above all others, and it was for him, I would endure all that Marko Korelesk wanted.

Each moment in this room, in this building, was part of a grand plan. I was here to ensure the doors flung open when his army knocked upon the gates.

For my son, I would do all that was necessary to save his throne.

I parted from Kenan though it broke the old man's heart.

"I understand," he muttered. "It is something you must do."

"I have no choice."

"We all have choices. Sometimes, they do not appear to be so, but always, there is an option to turn another way."

Kenan walked away and did not return to his posting at the front door. In fact, I was the last to see him, the last to watch him disappear amongst the roses in the garden.

My grief was short-lived for the King kept me distracted. When I was not with him, I was selecting clothes, purchasing jewelry, and setting my hair.

Although, I was not to be Queen, I was giving free reign and an allowance to do as I pleased.

"You are the queen of my heart," Marko declared, pulling me close to his rotund chest. "But, I have chosen not to wed again after the death of both my son and wife."

That was fine with me, for I did not love Marko even a little. Pleasing him was a dreadful chore, in which I would always close my eyes and dream of someone else.

Who? Certainly, not Pellen, nor Kenan, and there were no other lovers, save one. Only Mikal came to mind, and even then, it was hardly an act of love, but a duty of a young woman to her king.

Afterwards, as Marko lay in bed, he would recite a never ending litany of complaints.

"The people are fools! They do not respect me as they should. Why do they act as if I feed them all? Do they not have hands and feet with which they may work? If they want coins from me, they must join my army. Yet, the Generals tell me there is few men willing to fight and fewer still who are healthy or able to shoot a gun. And, if that wasn't enough, they are refusing to pay the tithes I have imposed. Fortunately, I have camps where my work is done by Karut slaves."

I would cluck and murmur false sounds of comfort, while my heart burned, for I had known those camps well. Did he forget that is where he found me only a few years ago? Did he forget that the blood of the motherland filled my veins, that I was one of those whom he scorned?

One day, the King came to me in a rage and no amount of comfort would calm his angry heart, as he stormed back and forth across the room.

"The Karuts! I wish every one of them dead. They have the gall to strike at our shoreline cities, burning them, creating chaos, killing those who dare to fight. Terrorists, they are! Do they think they can turn my country into ash? I will capture those foolish young men and all within my reign who dare to aide them. I will hang them by their necks outside these palace walls."

Now, I grew fearful, and I wondered if and when he tired of me, would I also hang with them?

"I will kill that young one myself," Marko declared.

"What young one?" I gasped, before immediately lowering my voice.

Disguising my alarm, I reached for my hairbrush and briskly, pulled it through my hair. Marko loved when my hair shone like polished gold. He would wrap his fingers around it, tugging it only a little too hard.

"A young fool," the King waved his hand through the air, "not even fully grown. The Karuts call him their prince, their new MaKennah, even though King Rekah has no true born son."

"A boy," I scoffed, my voice choked and far too high, when finally I was able to utter a word. "Do not worry after a boy. You have an army with guns and trucks and ships, while the Karuts have nothing but swords and horses."

Marko made a snorting noise and spittle flew from his thick lips. "I shall have him brought here to my palace and I shall see his body hanging from the flagpole in the courtyard. Like a flag he will be, and a warning to all. Let them see how I treat traitors who conspire against my reign."

The autumn arrived again and with it fierce winter-like storms. The ocean pounded against the rocks and the seawall, as if it's only desire was to break it down. Rain fell from the sky for days, intermingled with enormous rocks of hail. Within weeks of the end of summer, it began to snow, far earlier than ever before.

Then, the winds came, terrible gales that howled day and night. Unceasingly, they pounded the windows as if demanding to either come in, or blow the building down.

"The angels are angry still," the maids of the palace whispered in the shadows. "Something terrible will happen soon. The winds foretell it. They always do."

I agreed, but did not breathe a word. A dark foreboding washed over me, accompanied by a malaise that made me weak. Every morning, my stomach churned and rejected all food, leaving me to do nothing, but lay exhausted in my bed, until the hours before dusk when I managed to rise.

"Be ready," Grandmother called from the back of my brain when I dawdled, unable to convince my feet to touch the floor. "The times will quickly change. The pendulum swings again, back and forth. Do not lay about like a weakling when you must be strong."

"Hush Grandmother!" I snapped, just as a branch scratched against the window of my room. My outburst startled the maid who was straightening the fine silken sheets around me.

"Sorry, Ma'am." She lowered her eyes, a blush creeping up her face. Surely, she thought me insane, addressing a wayward branch as if it was my grandmother.

With a half curtsy, suitable for a woman who wasn't quite the Queen, the maid disappeared into the closet to fetch a robe for me to wear.

There were little, save a robe that fit me well these days. Although in the mornings, my stomach rebelled, by the afternoon, I was famished and ate most anything.

I had added weight and my belly had grown round with fat. My skin and hair shone, such that everyone remarked how beautiful this new plump figure looked upon me.

Marko heard this and at first, he glowed with pride, but later, his mouth grew tight with jealousy for the compliments I received. In fact, it seemed as if daily his mood worsened, along with the weather. Each report of a Karut strike upon our cities filled him with rage.

He was sleeping little, I knew, for the storms were forever roaring just outside. If that were not enough, the perimeter of the palace was surrounded by people day and night. They begged for food and called for help, gathering about fires made in old tin drums, some demanding Marko's ouster, as if this was all his doing.

Coming upon me now while the maid was still in the closet, Marko stood before my bed and raised his hand.

"Why are you still lying about?" he roared. "Get up, you lazy Karut!" He struck me across the cheek, before turning away to pace across the room.

"Marko!" I gasped, tears quickly filling my eyes. My head swam as I made to sit upright, my jaw aching.

"Don't call me that, you Karut witch! Address me as your king and lord."

"Why are you so angry at me, m'lord?" I begged. "What I have done to so displease you that you strike me, I, your loving and humble servant?"

"The Karut Prince!" he declared, turning on heel to rush at me again. He came to my bedside and glared at me, as if he knew the truth inside my heart.

Although my blood pounded in my ears, I held my tongue and lowered my eyes.

"What of him?"

"I had a dream of him." Marko's smile turned into an ugly sneer. "He came to me in my bed and with a knife he held to my throat, he told me he would return to claim his throne. Never!" Marko spun around. "I will kill him with my bare hands before he takes my crown." Then, Marko hit me upon my head with such a force that I was thrown to the floor. He kicked me and spat upon me, cursing me, and all my brethren. "Soon, you shall see him and all his warriors swinging by their necks, for we have captured them, and will hang them from these gates."

"No!" I wept, as Marko stormed away.

"Can I help you, Mistress?" the maid whispered, kneeling by my side.

"No."

I refused to move. I refused to leave the safety of the floor. I had to think. I had to decide what my next course of action was to be. Surely Marko would kill me too if he knew who had birthed his enemy prince. I had to do something before the both of us ended up dead.

I needed to flee, but to where and how would I go in this condition when I could barely rise from my bed or walk ten steps. Was there anyone in the palace who would protect me, who would rescue me and my son?

"Grandmother, help me!" I called to the air.

"You are safe," Grandmother replied. "Your protector is in your womb waiting for his birth. As to the other, send for the old man. Bid him bring the boy to your nephew who lives amongst the stars. Let him wait until it is time for him, for once again, the pendulum will swing back and forth."

Chapter 23
Dov

We arrived on the shores of the Mishnese continent in nearly the same place from which Amyr and I had originally departed. It was a bittersweet reunion for me, returning to the country of my birth, the land of my fathers, but also the land I had fled.

We arrived in the night, swimming ashore from the boat, which immediately departed on sails as silent as the wind. Afterward, we hid beneath the docks, drying our clothes, resting, and praying that we would accomplish what we had been sent to do.

No prayers would come to my lips though. Instead, all I could think on was Amyr and his words to me. I was the phoenix, not him. I was the one would save my people and restore this planet. I wore this on my arm and carried this vision in my heart. This time, I was the master and he, my loyal servant. This time, I would be the king, not him.

We began by lighting a fire at the wharf, igniting empty buildings, abandoned fisherman's shacks and piles of rubbish. Like a long fuse twisting and turning, our path of fires crawled across the city, the final point of detonation, still unknown.

From there, we spread outward setting blazes at every stop, so that by the time the winter came, Farku's skies were permanently darkened by thick clouds. An acrid haze hung like fog across the entire region, despite how the winds might try to blow it away.

The King's forces couldn't stop us, for we worked quickly and disappeared long before the morning light. We were shadows in the dark, silent fireflies instantly stinging and flying away.

Each morning, we would rendezvous in the woodlands, recounting our adventures and planning the next, eating whatever we found and sleeping wherever we could manage to shelter.

Never did we lack for fire, even if the rain had soaked all our tinder through. Amyr could make fire in his hands, enough to light even the most recalcitrant torch.

"How does he do that?" the other boys asked me. "From nothing, he creates fire in the air."

"It is said the Great Emperor had that skill as well," Bear whispered. "Amyr is the MaKennah reborn."

"He is not," I declared. "He has said as much himself. I am the one who has returned to be the savior."

Of course, they all laughed at this. Little Dov was no bigger than a child, while Amyr could have been the Great Emperor's twin.

I showed them, though. I became the best firesetter of anyone. Amyr would give me a torch and like a bolt of lightning, I would race to my target and set it blazing.

I came to love the scent of smoke and relish the warmth of the white hot flames. Sparks drifting into the sky at night became more beautiful to me than a galaxy of stars.

Each time I set the first match, backing away to the shadows as the inferno rose, a thrill would race down my spine, filling me with a euphoric joy. The fire became my addiction, the flames an intoxicating drug that possessed my soul. I forgot about Lorinda. I forgot about everything except the compulsion to set the flames alight again, and each day became a trial while I waited for the night.

In the autumn when the storms raged as angry as if it was the height of winter, instead of returning to our hideout in the woods, Amyr took me into a town.

"Where are we going?" I demanded, watching my latest blaze recede from view. "Where are the others? Is this our new meeting place?"

At first, Amyr didn't respond, although I saw a thin smile cross his lips.

"It is time you learned to love something other than fire," he said, leading me into the house.

There, he left me in the care of a woman much older than myself and with a skill that made my fire-setting pale in comparison.

"We must leave. Hurry, Dov." Amyr pulled me from a dream.

I had been asleep in a bed beneath silken sheets and blanket filled with warm soft down. It had been years since I slept in a bed as fine as this, one worthy of my grandfather's ducal manor house, but with the added benefit of a beautiful naked woman by my side.

"Join us, Amyr," the woman said, holding out her hand. "Or, better yet, let me leave your little friend to another girl, while you and I go off to somewhere else."

Amyr smiled and his odd eyes glowed.

"Next time," he murmured, placing a cigarette upon his lip.

"My girls treated you well?"

"I am satiated."

"You are never satiated," she protested, sitting upright so he could see her magnificent breasts.

"Why have you come, Amyr?" I snapped, noting his hesitation. "Didn't you just say that you and I have to leave?"

"I did."

He nodded to me, before somewhat reluctantly, turning on heel. The door closed behind him, followed by his footsteps hurrying down the hall.

"Go on, child," the woman called me, even though Amyr and I were nearly of the same age. She pushed me from the bed and so, quickly, I found my clothing and hurried from the room.

I felt taller. I felt older. I felt like I needed to light a dozen fires, after which, I would return to purchase another girl.

A few minutes later, I met Amyr in the doorway where he was finishing his cigarette. An old man stood in the street stroking the mane of an equally old mule. Behind them, waited a cart covered by a ragged canopy and filled with all sorts of goods, including skins, buckets of wheat and bottles of ale.

"Get in." Amyr motioned in the direction of the cart. Then, he tossed his spent cigarette into the air, and immediately, produced another.

"What of the others?" I asked, climbing into the cart, lying flat upon the wooden slats, as the canopy wasn't tall enough for even me to sit upright.

Amyr joined me, laying side by side, and we began to bounce to the slow, but steady rhythm of the mule's gait.

"Last night, they were captured by the Korelesk army. They have been taken to the Capitol City where they will hang."

I started to say we must do something, but caught my tongue before uttering such useless words. What could we do, set fire to the palace? Undoubtedly, by the time we arrived in this mule cart, our friends would be dead. It was only because Amyr took me to the whorehouse that I was still alive.

"You are the savior, Dov," Amyr whispered, although I thought I heard a smirk in his voice. "If you wish to do something, then, do it."

I was. I was the firesetter. I was also the only grandson of the Duke of Kildoo. If I killed Marko Korelesk, whose claim to the throne was no better than mine, I could be King of Mishnah and King of Karupatani. I could be the new Emperor.

"We will burn down the Imperial Palace," I decided.

Amyr laughed. "It is made of stone."

"Then, we will sneak in and kill Marko Korelesk in his bed."

Amyr shrugged and blew a cloud of thick gray smoke into the air. After which, he flicked away his cigarette and yawned heavily, rolling to his side.

"I didn't sleep last night," he said, almost instantly starting to snore.

I stayed awake plotting and planning what I would do. In my mind, I killed the King a thousand times. I imagined myself upon his throne, the Great Emperor's crown of gold upon my head. I would declare Lorinda, the farmer's daughter, as my queen, and Amry would stand behind me, always ready to repel any attack.

I wouldn't need an army. Amyr, with the fire in his fingers and his foresight, would protect me better than a hundred men. I would reward him for this. I would make everyone treat him almost as if he was the king, but no one would forget that the savior, the new MaKennah was really me.

My bravado was short-lived when we arrived in the Capitol City the following week. Amyr and I left the carter at the river's edge and walked the remaining distance to the palace. Snow had fallen the night before leaving the air so frigid it chilled my bones despite the heavy cloak and fur boots upon my feet.

Amyr was unfazed by either the cold, or the crowds of people in the streets.

"A coin to spare?" a boy asked me, holding out his hand as we walked by. I had none, but Amyr had a purse-full, although he didn't share.

"Sorry," I told the boy and every other one who asked the same, while thinking not long ago, I was just like him.

"Get over it, Dov," Amyr snapped, replying to my silent thoughts, as we entered a crowd of people gathered around the palace gates. They were whispering amongst themselves, pointing and shoving each other closer so all might see.

"What is it?" I whispered to Amyr. "What is there?"

I failed to hear Amyr's response as a large woman shoved me away in her effort to join the front of the crowd. After that, I couldn't see over or around anyone to find my lost friend. A few times, I called his name, but my voice was trampled by the shouting and the jeers. Still, we moved forward as a pack, bodies crammed together side by side.

As we neared the palace gates, the shouting changed to *Ooohs* and *Aaahs*.

"What is it?" I asked my neighbor.

"Look up, boy."

I followed the woman's finger as she pointed at the pikes above the fence. There hung four men, dangling by their necks.

"Serves them right, dirty Karuts," the woman hissed, her sentiments echoed by the crowd, while I did my best not faint, or to spew upon her shoes.

There hung Turak, Borak, Pori and Bear, recognizable by the thick black hair, which covered his head and naked body like a coat.

"They say these are the ones that burned Farku," a man murmured. "The firesetters who turned that city into ash."

"Let them burn!" another cried, while I slipped behind him, pushing all aside, reaching for a place where no one else would be standing.

When I was freed of the crowd, I ran. Heading back to the river, I followed it through the old city and into the woods. Amyr was lost to me in the crowd. I would never find him and neither was I certain that I wished to.

He had brought me here. He had taken me from Lorinda and the village. He had brought upon all these boys a horrific, ghastly death.

That night, as I hid inside a fallen log, sheltering from the endless gales of ice and snow, I realized I was not the firesetter after all. I could not summon flames to my fingers. Only Amyr could do that. Whatever I had done, whatever I would do, would be at his behest. It had always been this way, and it would always be. If I was to become the king, it would only be if Amyr had decided I should sit his throne.

With nowhere else to go and the motherland too far away and across the sea, I followed the winds, which blew north in the direction of Kildoo.

Weeks later, I arrived at my grandfather's door, collapsing into his serving woman's arms.

"*'Tis* like seeing a ghost, I am. Ye are the spittin' image of the late Duke's son and ye arrived just in time to see yer granddad's body laid to rest."

"Then, I am the Duke now," I declared and so, I was, and would remain, until Amyr disappeared, leaving me alone to challenge Marko Korelesk.

Chapter 24
Ailana

On the eve of the winter solstice when the snows had piled in drifts as high as tall man's head, and the wind howled against the windows demanding entry, I thrashed about in my bed, a victim of horrific dreams. Outside and below me, hanging from the palace gates were the bodies of four men, boys from the motherland, kinsmen to me, sharing my blood and the blood of my two sons.

Inside, their spirits haunted my room. Ghostly shadows flew in circles above my head.

"Ailana," they called out my name. "You have forgotten who you are."

"I am the mother of the next king," I declared. "Go away. Leave me be."

"You forsake your kinsmen for your own benefit. You shall reap the seeds of your betrayal."

"Ailana," Grandmother whispered. "You disappointment me."

"No," I begged. "Please leave me alone!"

"Mistress?" the maid said, shaking my arm.

Instantly, the ghosts departed and it was only the wind whistling through the room, which called my name.

"What is it?" I demanded, coming to my senses.

The maid leaned close to my ear, her sour breath, invading my nostrils with the scent of failing teeth.

"The Karut Prince has been captured. The guards found him outside watching his kinsman swing."

"Are you certain it is he?" I gasped, already knowing the answer before she spoke.

"I saw him, Mistress. He was dragged through the courtyards, through the snow. The King intends to hang him from the flagpole next to the icicle fountain."

"In this weather?" I gasped, as my mind refused to grasp what was soon to be.

"Come see for yourself, Mistress. The King summons you to watch the poor lad's body swing."

"I won't," I cried, refusing to leave my bed, though curiosity demanded my own eyes confirm what I knew to be true.

"*'Tis* an order, Mistress. His Majesty says if you refuse, he'll send the guard to string you up beside him. You are kinsmen in blood, if not more than that."

I had no choice. Laboriously, I climbed from the bed, my heavy body unyielding, refusing to bend, even to slip the boots upon my feet.

"I'll help you, Mistress," the maid insisted. "*T'won't* be long now 'afore yer prince arrives."

She wrapped my warmest cloak about my shoulders and placed my boots. Then, with her arm as a cane to guide my way, we left the safety of my suite for the palace corridors. Snow and ice lined our path, for the walkways were without glass and exposed to the elements.

"Mistress," the King declared when I arrived at his side on the landing above the snow-laden courtyard.

There directly below me was a boy whose face was as familiar to me as my own. Though he was older by many years, I saw only the child I had held to my breast.

"He favors Mikal, doesn't he?" Marko sneered. "And, the Great Emperor before him. Those Karut genes are strong. But, I see nothing of you in him. Perhaps, his bitch was another of Mikal's whores?"

"Amyr," I wept, as the noose was placed around my son's neck.

"Look at him, Karut," Marko ordered, putting his hand around my own neck. "Watch him die. That is your punishment for today. A bastard whelp of Mikal and an adopted son of Rekah shall not claim the Imperial Throne which belongs to me."

I lifted my eyes and with them, I tried to tell my son to be strong.

"Fight, Amyr," I whispered just as thunder roared above our heads and a bolt of lightning seared across the sky. It struck the icicle fountain, and with a tremendous crack, split the glass masterpiece into a million jagged shards.

Like thunder, the sound of the glass bursting echoed across the facades of all the buildings, just as the wind rushed into the courtyard, howling and moaning as the ghosts had in my dreams. The gales seized upon the shards, whirling them upward in a lethal tornado before raining them upon all who stood in the courtyard below.

It was then amongst the screams and chaos of this deadly storm that the flames of fire arose from the buildings of the palace.

"This can't be!" Marko raged. "This palace can't burn. It is crafted entirely from marble and stone."

But, he was wrong for even the hardest granite could melt if consumed by a fire as hot as that which burned in Hell.

Marko left me, racing across the hallways to the stairs, saving himself for he cared not for any other.

"Come, Mistress," the maid cried, urgently pulling at my arm, leading me through the clouds of smoke and fields of glass to the ocean's shore.

By the time, we were far enough away so the heat did not burn the hair from our heads or skin from our faces, my belly lurched and cramped. Water ran down my legs, followed by a tremendous pain. Now, I could move no more. I collapsed in the snow, my blood ushering in the arrival of my second son.

As I clutched him to my breast and fed him his first meal, only briefly did I mourn the death of his brother, Amyr. Surely, he had not survived the carnage in the courtyard, especially with his hands bound and a noose around his neck.

But, I had. I had lived to give birth to another boy, a new prince with no taint or question upon his claim, for here was my new son, Marek Korelesk, prince and heir to the Imperial Throne.

Chapter 25
Lance

We had just delivered a load of coconuts to Spacebase 44-C, when Taul and I were sitting in the cockpit playing cards. The ship was running well and the endless stars were pretty dull, so I was dealing out a hand of Gin Rummy while Taul was keeping score.

Taul had been part of crew for more than a year and I considered him a decent space sailor even though he had only trained on freighters like the Flying Mule. Because he lacked SpaceForce experience, initially, I wouldn't let him have a gun, until I caught him shooting targets with Sandy at a spacebase sim center.

That made me realize he was a pretty good shot, maybe even better than me, and certainly better than Wen or Noodnick, who couldn't hit the side of building from five feet away. Sandy was a good marksman, too, a skill she must have inherited from her mother. Jill had been known to shoot just as accurately with both hands, which wasn't the only thing her hands had been famous for.

At any rate, Taul and I were slapping down cards and chewing the fat, when I must have realized that in our course to Altaris II, we were passing the star system that was once home to the old Empire. I pointed that out in between dealing a new hand and fetching sodas from the fridge.

"I know," Taul replied. "That's where I am from."

"Really?" I hadn't known that. Frankly, I hadn't known anything about Taul, other than, like I said, he worked on freighters like the Mule. "Sandy has an old Imperial coin of mine. I was once told it might be worth a whole lot of money."

"I can take a look at it," Taul offered, tipping back his soda. "I had some coins too when I came to the Alliance. Until I got my first job, this was how I managed to eat."

"So, how did you come here?" I asked, noting a ship off our starboard bow. It was moving slowly, too slowly to be SpaceForce, or an industrial freighter.

Taul shrugged and slapped down a perfect Gin.

"There are still old ships and old skippers around for hire. I had a guy take me to the nearest spacebase. Anything can be bought for the price of a few gold coins. Your bid, Captain."

"Pass," I said and turned to track that ship.

Either unintentionally, or by design, it seemed to be traveling on a perpendicular vector with us. Eventually, it sped up, so it was on a path for a direct collision unless we turned. In space, a hundred miles away was considered breathing down your neck. This guy was practically within spitting distance of my bow, which made me really nervous when we crossed paths. I had to brake so suddenly, it caused all our cargo to go flying, slamming into the walls of the hold.

"Who is driving this thing?" We heard Wen shout from the aft cabin.

"Asshole!" I screamed, pounding the console with my fist.

"Who? Wen?" Taul asked, reaching for the cards, soda bottles and chips which I inadvertently sent tumbling to the floor.

"Where in the hell does he think he's going? With all this space around, why the fuck did he cut me off? I'm going to follow him."

"Who, Daddy?" Sandy asked, opening the cockpit door.

She was dressed in pajamas and her hair was piled on top of her head. Fortunately, it was no longer black, but the brilliant auburn of her birth. Her big green eyes were half closed and she was scratching at a zit that had erupted on her chin. Other than that, I still considered her the most beautiful creature I had ever seen.

"That guy." Taul pointed at the ship, which we could now see was a tiny passenger vessel, maybe even some rich guy's private plane. Except it was old, really old.

"That's an ancient Imperial spaceplane," Sandy yawned, "Hard to believe that any of those are still flying."

"There's a few still," Taul said. "Although, I don't think his range is very far. He'll probably have to stop at Spacebase 43 to regenerate his fuel. That may be why he's in such a hurry. It could be his engine is about to die."

"Alright," I announced, setting the Flying Mule on a new course. "We'll follow him there, just in case his plane conks out. It's the law of the stars, you know. We're going to save a fellow traveler in distress and if he makes it without a problem, when we get to the spacebase, I'm going to punch him in the nose."

I didn't know if I would really punch him in the nose, but at the time, it sounded good. Frankly, if he turned out to be an eight-foot tall Cascadian with three rows of shark-like teeth, I'd probably turn and run.

In the meantime, I didn't mind making an extra pitstop, as the Flying Mule was showing an anomaly on her gear oil gauges. One of them was reading hot, while the other was reading cold. The transmission pressure was also a little off which may or may not have been related.

Without alarming anyone, especially Wen, who always assumed we were about to die, I figured we'd get the Mule checked out and have a nice dinner at the best little steakhouse restaurant in space.

Several hours later, we pulled into the docking bay to do exactly that.

The ancient Imperial spaceplane was in the slip beside us and two men were standing right outside, one of them smoking a cigarette.

As I debarked the Mule and went to check the thru-hulls, I heard Taul shout. He bolted down the ladder after me and ran to the guy with the smoke. The two of them hugged, sort of, and clapped each other on the back.

"Maybe, his friend," Wen suggested, gazing up at the dripping hydraulic fluid which was leaking from the ship.

"Well, since he's obviously not an eight-foot Cascadian, I guess I have to hold to my word and punch him in the nose. Cutting us off back there probably cracked our whole load of coconuts."

Leaving Wen to deal with the mechanical issues, I headed across the bay to Taul and his buddy, who was standing with an old man.

I didn't punch anyone. I wouldn't hit an old guy for his reckless driving. Furthermore, Taul was very excited to introduce me to his cousin, who coincidentally, was looking for a job.

"Do you think he could join our crew, Captain Lancelot?" Taul practically begged me to take his cousin on, even though he had no recent experience in working in space, or anywhere else, for that matter. "I will vouch for him. I guarantee he will be useful to our crew."

I wasn't so sure about that. The guy looked sleepy, or maybe, he looked stoned. His eyes were only half open, just thin little slits, which seemed to sparkle with color. He also looked young, probably too young to get a space license. There was also something familiar about him. I could have sworn I had seen his face before.

"We could use another crewman," Wen added, now sniffing at the hydraulic fluid on his fingers.

"I will train him," Taul assured me.

It was then that I realized where I had seen him. He was the guy whose face was on my old Imperial coin.

Unfortunately, I had no time to consider this and what it meant, as Noodnick appeared on the boarding steps jumping up and down. He made a noise. A screech, similar to a primal wail, until his mouth stretched and twisted trying to say a single word.

"What Nood?" Wen asked. "What's the matter? Tell us slowly."

"Sandy!" Noodnick pronounced, the first words ever to be uttered from his mouth. "Sandy has a run away."

The Firesetter series continues with book 2
Amyr's Command

Find it exclusively on Amazon.com

http://www.amazon.com/dp/B01295478E

Would you like to join my mailing list and hear all about my new releases as well as get updates on great book sales, and occasionally a recipe that I like?

If so, sign up here:

http://eepurl.com/bLz0lT

If you enjoyed *A Thread of Time*, please be sure to leave me some love on Amazon.com.
Your reviews are very much appreciated.

Printed in Great Britain
by Amazon